Tales of the Were
Jaguar Island 1

The Jaguar Tycoon

BIANCA D'ARC

Copyright © 2017 Bianca D'Arc
Published by Hawk Publishing, LLC

Copyright © 2017 Bianca D'Arc

All rights reserved.

ISBN: 197980303X
ISBN-13: 978-1979803038

It all started at dinner…

Mark is the larger-than-life billionaire Alpha of the secretive Jaguar Clan. Business tycoon and man about town, he's the guest of honor at a huge society dinner in lower Manhattan. Shelly is at the dinner to network and possibly find some clients for her architectural design business. She comes from old money, but her family has fallen on hard times in recent decades and she likes to work for her living.

A violent beginning to a magical destiny…

When a man she'd been chatting with starts shooting at Mark, Shelly is dragged to a back room for questioning. When Shelly and Mark meet face to face, something changes forever. Her fate tangles with his as he introduces her to a world she never knew existed. A world where men turn into huge predatory cats and magic is real.

Can the Alpha's dream come true?

Commissioning Shelly to design a community on the private island Mark just purchased is a way to keep her close. It'll be up to the Alpha jaguar to convince her that they are meant to be, and to keep her safe from his enemies. Or will it be her keeping him safe? Stranger things have happened…

DEDICATION

This one is for my loyal friends and readers. I hope you enjoy this new branch of shifters.

I want to thank my editor, Jess Bimberg, for doing a super-quick turnaround. She really went above and beyond the call of duty this time and I can't thank her enough. Special thanks to Peggy McChesney for her help in finding typos and things that just didn't make any sense! LOL.

This project had some delays, including unexpected surgery earlier in the year that caused a very big postponement. I'm so happy to have survived my bout with uterine cancer and still be here to complete this project...and many more to come. So that's a big thank you to God for giving me a second chance.

And a thank you to all my fans, family, and friends who took the time to send me messages of support and encouragement when I was so very scared and in pain. I survived. With the best possible outcome. I'm cured and hoping to live a long, healthier life in the future with lots more books and lots and lots of love.

PROLOGUE

The gunman jumped up from his seat at one of the many dinner tables in the elegant hall and began firing. Mark ducked, even as he felt the near miss of a bullet go whizzing past his head. He narrowed his eyes, looking toward his security team. He'd jump in if he had to, but in such a public setting, he really had to at least pretend to be human.

He scrambled off the podium, surrounded by a few of his people, allowing himself to be whisked away into an anteroom while others dealt with the threat. He didn't like it. His inner predator longed to go take a bite out of the jackass that dared attack him and put others in danger.

But he couldn't do that. Not here, in such a public place. Not with so many witnesses.

In private, though... There, he could be the Alpha he truly was. And heaven help the bastard who had just tried to shoot him.

CHAPTER 1

"You want to tell me why your boyfriend just tried to blow away my employer?"

The bodyguard's face was a little too handsome for such work, Shelly decided. With the way he was barking at her, he should have a scar running down one cheek and an eye patch at the very least. Maybe a hook for a hand and a parrot on his shoulder, too.

But, no. Both hands looked intact, though there were calluses. Finally! A flaw in Attila the Bodyguard. She didn't like him, but she could still appreciate how good looking all the people surrounding Mark Pepard were. It was kind of freakish. Not only was Pepard a gorgeous billionaire, but he surrounded himself with beautiful hard-bodies. Maybe he had some kind of fetish and didn't hire normal-looking people. She marveled that he hadn't been sued for discrimination yet, if that was the case.

"He's not my boyfriend." She'd been saying that over and over, but Attila hadn't seemed to get the message. He might be handsome, but she suspected he was stupid. Typical.

"Security footage shows you arriving together in the same cab and chatting throughout the party. Until about ten minutes before he pulled a gun on my employer. Sure looks like you were together."

"We shared a cab. We struck up a conversation. He seemed interesting and wanted to keep talking to me. Since I didn't know anybody else at the reception, I figured I'd chat with him a while. I had no idea he was hell bent on getting himself arrested by attacking one of the richest men in the known universe."

She was getting fed up with being alternately yelled at and insulted by this man. He'd been at it for hours now. Hours. Ever since the party had been interrupted by a failed assassination attempt by the man from the cab.

Shelly really didn't know the guy. He'd just been a stranger who happened to be going to the same place. She'd offered to share the cab, which had been her first mistake. Talking to the man for an hour had been the second. And the third had been going with Mr. Hard Ass Bodyguard when he'd silently escorted her out of the reception hall.

At the time, she'd had no idea what had happened, but they'd showed her the tape a few times now, and she realized the rather clumsy assassination attempt had been quickly defused by efficient and professional bodyguards. Most likely, very few people at the party even realized anything untoward had occurred. They'd whisked her out of there so quickly, her head had spun.

The reception and dinner party had been a charity event held in one of the oldest buildings on Wall Street. Her father had sent her as his representative, as he did to most of these kinds of things nowadays. She was his proxy in an empire that was slowly shrinking into obscurity.

Her father was from *old money*, as they called it. He'd never had to worry about saving, and the lifestyle he still lived echoed that mistaken belief. Shelly, though, had been born into the generation that had to work.

For the first time in a long time, a Howell actually had to work, but Shelly didn't mind. She knew her dad was blowing through whatever inheritance might be left, and she didn't begrudge him that. It was his money, inherited fair and square. Shelly preferred to make her own way.

She did, however, enjoy the elite party invites that he tossed her way. This evening, for example, posed a special treat. The old Customs House in downtown Manhattan was only opened for select events. Tonight had been her chance to study its architecture up close and personal. She would use it as inspiration for one of her clients, who wanted the same sort of old-world grandeur in the vacation getaway she was designing for him.

Shelly Howell was an architect. A *high society* architect, actually, given her family name and connections. There was increasing cachet to having her name on the plans for your new summer home or addition, in certain circles.

She didn't mind banking on the family name. Her father did the same—in a different way, of course. Few people really knew how fragile his empire had become. He got by on the perceived strength of his name in a lot of places, including the rubber chicken dinner circuit that he sent her on as his representative, as often as not.

Which was how she had ended up here, politely imprisoned in an antechamber of one of the oldest buildings in lower Manhattan. She had finished studying the construction and ornamentation of the plush room forty-five minutes ago, and was growing increasingly alarmed at the continued questioning.

"Look," she tried to reason with the man for the hundredth time. "My name is Shelly Howell. I drove down from Westchester last night to have dinner with a client. I checked into the Penn Hotel yesterday, so I wouldn't have to drive home and back again for the party tonight. I was there most of the day, working. When I asked the bellman to get me a taxi, he pointed out another guest who was going the same way and suggested we share because the rain was making cabs scarce. We did. End of story. I didn't know that man before the cab ride. I didn't have anything to do with his plan to hurt your boss. Now, either let me go or give me back my phone so I can call my lawyer."

The bastard bodyguard had the nerve to laugh. "I'm not

the police, honey. I don't have to give you a phone call. I can disappear you so you'll never be found, so don't fuck with me."

She gasped at the crude word and shot to her feet.

"You just try, you obnoxious bastard!"

The door clicked softly open, stopping her tirade before it could get going. She looked over, and there he was, the man of the hour. Mark Pepard. In the flesh.

His tuxedo jacket was missing, his bow tie draped around his neck, undone. It was a real bow tie. No clip-ons for this billionaire mogul, apparently.

"Leave her alone, Nick. She wasn't in on it."

He looked drunk, was her first thought as he strolled into the room and perched on the arm of the chair facing her. His eyes sparkled unnaturally, and his smile was lazy and...lecherous? *Oh, crap.*

"How are you so sure?" The bodyguard still looked skeptical.

"I just got back from her hotel. The room was clean. No sign of the man. And his room had no sign of her." His words were directed at the bodyguard he'd called Nick, but his eyes never left her. She felt like prey under the gaze of a deadly predator. "Don't you smell that? She's scared. And innocent."

Innocence has a scent? she wondered.

Shelly shook her head, trying to clear the sudden strange thoughts. She hadn't expected to get to meet the famous, and famously elusive, Mark Pepard, but she'd been wrong. She was looking at all six foot three of him, in a rumpled designer tuxedo.

Damn, he looked good enough to eat. Now where the heck had that thought come from?

She'd always thought he cut an elegant figure when she'd seen photos of him in various publications, from the financial magazines to celebrity gossip columns. He lived the high life to which her family was no longer strictly entitled. Actually, he lived higher than any Howell ever had. He was richer than the Queen of England, if the tabloids were to be believed, and he used his money in strange ways.

He was a daredevil, forever trying to break land speed records in his jet car. Or sail around the world by himself. Or fly into dangerous war-torn lands with no more than a single bodyguard and huge crates of relief supplies.

Damn. She just realized Nick was the bodyguard she'd seen by Pepard's side in those clandestine photos that had made their way into the tabloids. Scary Nick was his right-hand man. No wonder he'd seemed so familiar to her. Shelly admitted to herself that she'd been fascinated by those photos when they were leaked, and news of Pepard's hands-on philanthropy had changed her opinion of the playboy billionaire forever.

"So, Miss Howell, you're an architect?" His tone was friendly and conversational, as if his glowering friend over there hadn't just threatened to have her "disappeared." Was he insane as well as insanely wealthy? She decided to humor the possible lunatic.

"Yes, I am. I suppose you saw some of my work in my hotel room?" She was appalled that he'd been in her room, but if it had convinced him of her innocence, she wasn't going to quibble.

"I did," he confirmed with a slight grin. "And you have quite an eye for design, if I'm any judge. I'd like you to consider doing some work for me, if you can forgive my friend's rather…uh…overzealous questioning here tonight." Only then did his gaze flick briefly to the bodyguard as the man backed away, only a foot or so, but giving her a little breathing space.

Did she want to work for Mark Pepard? That was a no brainer. Who *didn't* want to work for one of the richest men in the world? A few hours ago, she would have jumped at the chance, but those few intervening hours had changed a lot about her perception of the man and his hirelings.

She looked from Mark to Nick and back again, uncertainly. "I'm not sure. I'd need to hear more about the project first."

Mark surprised her by laughing at her caution. She had been afraid he would be offended, but he was taking her trepidation better than she'd expected. She imagined few people said no to him.

"Of course. You've had a rather rude introduction to me and my people. We're going to have to work hard to change your opinion of us." He stood from his perch on the arm of the chair and walked up to her. He came close. Almost too close. She had to crane her neck upward to meet his mesmerizing gaze. "I'm sorry we scared you, Shelly. Nick is naturally protective of me, which I count as a good thing, but in this instance, I could wish he'd gone a little easier on you. I don't want my future mate afraid of me."

"Your what?" Had she heard him right?

"Mark?" Nick spoke at nearly the same moment as she did, confusion and concern clear in his tone.

"You both heard me." Mark's smile was for her alone as he gazed deep into her eyes. She felt drugged by his presence, unable to move, even as he stepped closer and caught her in his arms. "You two are going to have to learn to get along," he whispered as his lips dropped to hers, claiming her in a kiss that she should not have allowed but was powerless to resist.

Mark purred as he kissed his woman. Purred. In human form. Lady Bless! What he had suspected when he'd first scented her was true. She was his destined mate. The woman he had searched every continent to find...and here she was. In his arms at last.

The wave of recognition and longing that had hit him when he first entered her hotel room had only gotten more urgent the longer he breathed the air that still held her scent. He had lifted her garments out of her overnight bag and sniffed the heady aroma of his woman.

At last. At long last.

Then, anger had filled him as he remembered why he was

there. He'd stalked to the would-be assassin's room, sniffing loudly and not caring who heard or saw him. His men surrounded him, and he knew they wondered at his silent anger, but he had no words for them. He wouldn't be satisfied until he'd sniffed every last article in the man's room and was certain there was not even the faintest trace of his mate on the other man's things.

To think she would betray him was a dagger through his heart. He didn't breathe easy until he was certain there was no lingering connection between her and the man who had tried to shoot him.

There wasn't. Praise the Mother of All. Mark didn't need that kind of complication on top of everything else. His mate was innocent.

And human.

And totally unaware of what he was, or that his kind even existed.

But the man who'd tried to kill him had known. The bastard's gun had been loaded with silver bullets. More specifically, silver hollow points, packed with powdered pure silver dust. Poison to his kind. Being shot by one of those bullets would have guaranteed an agonizing death.

That thought alone allowed him to break the kiss and step away. He had to play this game, and play it well. She didn't know what she was dealing with, and someone very dangerous was gunning for him. Not the man who'd shared her cab. He was just a pawn in a much larger game.

But the one who'd sent him had known when and where to strike. The attack had been designed to either kill Mark or make him expose himself. Few shifters could control their transformation when in the extreme agony of silver poisoning. Mark could, but few realized just how powerful an Alpha he truly was.

His enemy knew Mark was a shifter but was still probing to find out how strongly his beast rode him. This little feint had all the earmarks of a test. Fortunately, his men had neutralized the threat before it had reached him. With any luck, the enemy was still in the dark about the extent of Mark's abilities—although they had no doubt learned to respect those Mark kept around him as security.

The next feint would not be so bold, nor so easy to evade. The thought sent a chill through Mark's blood, effectively cooling his head enough to think of his mate's welfare.

"Miss Howell, forgive me. I know you are neither easy nor likely to give yourself to me for selfish reasons. I will put no pressure on you in that way, rest assured, but there is a deeper game afoot here than you realize. First, you need to know that I'm not entirely human."

"Mark!" Nick objected, as Mark had known he would. The first rule of being what they were was not to reveal themselves to the outside world. The secrecy of their kind had to remain sacrosanct.

The one exception was when one of their number found a mate among the humans. As Mark had just done.

Sweet Mother of All. He really, truly, had a mate, and she was standing right there, in front of him with disbelief and a bit of fear on her gorgeous face. He grimaced. It was going to get worse before it got better, but he had to believe the Mother of All would not have granted him a mate with a weak character. Shelly was going to learn some hard truths in the next few minutes, and how she reacted would tell him a great deal about how they would go on from here.

"Is the room secure?" Mark spared a quick glance for Nick, a hand signal telling his best friend to stand down.

"As secure as it can be off our home turf," Nick replied. The tilt of his head spoke volumes about his skepticism and worry over what Mark planned to do next.

"She needs to know." Mark gave Nick a longer look that said not to interfere.

"What do I need to know?" Shelly whispered, drawing his gaze back to her lovely face.

She was trembling, as she had been since he'd given in to desire and kissed her. Damn, she was beautiful and tasted so sweet... But he didn't have time to linger. Her introduction to their world was going to have to be brutally short, but there was no help for it.

"Watch and learn." He began to remove his clothing, and her eyes grew wide with alarm.

"What are you doing?" She moved back from him, probably fearing rape or worse.

He had to admit, he probably seemed like a madman at the moment, but there was no quicker way to prove he wasn't insane. He had to shift. And to shift, he had to get naked. She'd calm down—or not—after she realized what he was up to.

"Don't be afraid. You'll understand it all in a minute. I promise. And nobody's going to hurt you. Believe me, that's the last thing on my mind." He was bare-chested, and he liked the way her eyes followed his every move.

If he'd been the modest sort, he might've gone behind the couch to shuck his pants, but he'd never been especially reticent about getting naked in public, and he wanted her to see his body. He wanted her to see every last detail of the shift, so she'd believe it. He didn't want there to be any doubt in her mind that he was what he was. She had to know and believe.

Her life might very well depend on it.

Mark called the beast and let the magic take him. He held her gaze as his body began to change, welcoming the blissful agony of the half-shifted battle form and then letting it go, all the way to his beast form. Jaguar. Black as night and twice as deadly.

He stalked forward silently on four paws, scenting his mate. She didn't back away, and the beast liked her courage as he sniffed at the soft fabric of her dress. Other scents mingled on the fabric—cleaning chemicals, other people, the aromas of the food and drink that had been served at the party—but under it all was the warm, welcoming scent of his woman. The one the big cat recognized as his alone. The one the man inside the beast reveled in.

Her fingers reached out, and he placed his head under her

hand, loving the feel of her fingers running over his scalp. Then his back. She moaned, her scent full of confusion and...wonder? It was a good sign.

"That's enough, Mark." Nick's voice cut through the soft sound of her breathing.

She was nervous, but not afraid, and that gave him the strength to pull away from her touch. He'd showed her his beast to make her understand, but now, he had to talk to her as a man.

He stepped back from her and allowed the magic to overtake him once more.

CHAPTER 2

Shelly was in shock. One of the richest men in the world had just turned into a giant cat right in front of her. A…a leopard or jaguar…or something. It hadn't been a trick. She'd touched his fur. She'd felt the muscles rippling under the skin of his shoulders and upper back. He'd been warm and soft and so very masculine under her fingertips.

And now, he was facing her again, turning from furred beast into…naked man. Very naked man. Right in front of her. Sweet Mother in Heaven.

"You're…" She couldn't finish the sentence. She didn't even know what she'd intended to say.

"Not completely human. As I said. Now do you believe me?"

His smile could have charmed angels down from heaven. His body made her mouth water. And his unabashed confidence—all while sporting a raging and very impressive erection—made her want to know more about this intriguing…not *man*, surely. What was he?

"Half-cat? How is that even possible?" She didn't realize she'd spoken aloud until he laughed.

"Jaguar. Black jaguar, the rarest of our kind. Sacred in some circles. Revered among our brethren. I am the Alpha of our Clan."

Nick stepped forward, bending to retrieve Mark's pants along the way. He handed them to his boss and then took up an almost protective position at his side. His gaze gave away none of his thoughts. He was still Mr. Hard-Assed Bodyguard to her.

His eyes dared her to put a toe wrong. She didn't like him, but she began to see the resemblance between him and his employer. Could Nick become a giant jungle cat too? Somehow—incredible as it seemed—she began to believe he could.

Both were built on the massive side. Muscled. Sleek. Tall and bronzed as only men who spent a lot of time in the sun with their shirts off were. Mark had laugh lines around his inviting dark eyes. Nick's jaw clenched in hard, uncompromising lines as he stared at her with those ice blue eyes of his. His short hair was streaked with gold, kissed by the sun. Mark's was black as night, with a slight wave. Both were handsome as sin—as were the rest of Mark's people.

Nick stood guard as Mark bent to slip his pants on, not bothering with underwear. He didn't seem to be in any hurry to put away that impressive cock, but she was just as glad when it was hidden by the black fabric of his tuxedo pants. She could still see the bulge of it, of course, but he seemed just a little less threatening with it tucked behind the trappings of civility.

"Son of a bitch," she breathed aloud, realizing why. "All your staff. All those hard bodies and handsome faces. They're all like you, aren't they?"

"See, Nick? She's gorgeous and smart, too," Mark said to his bodyguard, almost playfully. The intense look he turned on her made her knees go weak. "I surround myself with my Clan. They're all fierce and loyal."

"If you have all of them, what do you want from me?" The whispered words found their way past her mouth. She was frightened, but also intrigued, and the internal censor that should have filtered the words between her brain and her mouth seemed to be offline for the moment.

"Everything, *querida*." His softly voiced words struck straight to her core. Mark stepped a foot closer to her, his dark eyes seeming to bore into her very soul. "My kind know their perfect match through scent. When I entered your hotel room, I was overwhelmed by the knowledge that I have searched the world over for you, and suddenly—without the slightest warning—here you are. I mean to make you mine for all time, Shelly. You will be my partner and mate, the mother to the next generation of black jaguar, if the Goddess wills. And I will be your faithful husband for as long as we both shall live."

Nick looked at his boss sharply. "Coming on a bit strong, aren't you, Mark?"

For the first time in her presence, the bodyguard cracked a smile. It changed his face. Made him seem human. She still didn't like him, but she would give him the benefit of the doubt. He certainly seemed to care about his boss. His…Alpha? Was that the word Mark had used?

Mark was walking, talking sex on a stick, but she didn't have a right to think about him in anything other than a professional capacity, despite the preposterous words he had just spoken. He was raving. He was nuts! He was…a jaguar? Were shapeshifters—like in the movies—real, after all?

Or was she just having some kind of psychotic episode?

Shelly sank to the couch behind her, knees trembling and hands clenched tightly together. She almost missed the seat, and would have if Mark hadn't sprung forward to catch and guide her. He sat gently next to her, taking her tightly clenched hands in his much larger grasp. Then, he rubbed her suddenly cold arms, and his dark eyes were full of concern when he tipped her chin upward so she had to look at him.

"Don't faint on me now, *querida*. You've been strong tonight so far. Be strong for a little while longer." His smile invited her to lean on him.

She didn't know what to do. Her gaze went around the room, looking for a way out, but there was only Mark and his meanie bodyguard.

"Kindness might kill her," Nick said, surprising her. "She needs your strength now, Alpha. She doesn't shrink from confrontation. She's stronger than she seems."

The mean guy's vote of confidence nearly floored her, but it did cause her chin to rise and her spine to stiffen just a bit. She'd stood strong in the face of Attila the Bodyguard's harsh questioning. No reason to let his boss's insanity turn her into quivering mush.

"I'm not sure what to say, Mr. Pepard." She tried to pull her hands out of his, but he wouldn't let go. His touch was gentle, though. He didn't force her, but he was also firm in his resolution to remain touching her. "I'll consider working for you, but anything else... Surely even you have to admit this is all a little sudden. Ten minutes ago, your bodyguard was all up in my face, threatening to make me disappear."

Mark looked up at Nick, a scowl on his face. "Nick, I'm shocked."

"No, you're not." Nick's easy manner with Mark spoke of a long friendship between the two—and an equality she wouldn't have guessed at before seeing them interact. "Until you arrived with your announcement, I thought she was a danger to you, Alpha. It's my job to keep you safe."

"And mine to watch out for you, as well," Mark said quietly. "The Alpha protects his Clan."

Shelly didn't understand any of this. It was too much to take in all at once. Only a few minutes ago, she'd been interrogated, and then, she'd seen something...something completely unbelievable. Her mind was in shock. Shelly shot to her feet, breaking Mark's hold on her hands.

"I'd like to go back to my hotel, please." She tried to put some fire behind her words, and apparently, she managed a reasonable facsimile.

Mark stood and tried to touch her, but she dodged his hands and went to stand by the door. She didn't know how far to push him, but so far, her bravado seemed to be working.

"I want to go now, if you don't mind." She resisted

tapping her foot impatiently. She didn't want to go overboard.

"*Querida*, don't you realize how serious I am? You are my mate. Don't ask me to let you go now that I've found you." Mark sounded genuine, but the whole notion still seemed insane to her. How could he claim such a thing when he didn't know all that much about her?

"I'm sure you're very serious, but so am I. You've given me a lot to think about. You have to realize there is no way I can give you an answer right now. I need time to adjust to…all of this. Before you…did what you just did…I had no idea such a thing was even possible."

"You overwhelmed her, Mark. Seriously," Nick shook his head, "you'd think you never dealt with a human before."

"I don't want her going back to that hotel. It's not safe." Mark seemed to give in, and the look on his face nearly broke her heart, but she had to remain strong. She had to get away from him. She needed to think.

"You have to. Think about how it would look if she didn't, Mark. The man who attacked you tonight was no doubt a pawn in a much larger game. They're going to be watching. She needs to carry on as if she is as innocent as she was when this evening started." Nick's eyes pinned her in place. "You can do that, right? Your life probably depends on behaving as you would normally, and not as if you learned that shapeshifters were real tonight."

"Normally, I'd have spent the night at the hotel and then driven home tomorrow. I just finished a project and have leads to follow up on when I get home," she admitted, thinking it through.

"No leads. Tomorrow, I will arrive at your home to discuss the work I want you to do for me," Mark said firmly. There was no arguing with Pepard when he got an idea in his head, or so the gossip said.

"And you will be guarded day and night," Nick put in. "You won't see them, but if you run into trouble, our people will be near enough to help, and to call in the cavalry, if needed."

"Who would bother me? I don't understand this at all."

Mark's expression was pained. She thought maybe she'd really hurt his feelings by wanting to get away, but she needed time—and space—to think.

"The Alpha has enemies," Nick explained. "All rich men do. But shapeshifters have more than most. There are many who want to kill us simply for what we are. Others want to try to control our power and our magic. Some want to study us or keep us as prizes or even pets."

"I'd like to see someone try that with me." Mark grinned, and he looked every inch the predator in that moment.

His expression sent a chill down her spine. This was a dangerous man. A dangerous beast. Both—in one handsome-as-sin package.

"The man who tried to shoot Mark tonight knew or guessed what we are. His gun was loaded with silver bullets. Silver is a deadly poison to us. If you have any silver jewelry, put it away. You won't be able to wear it around us. Gold is okay. Platinum is all right, too, but no silver. Understand?" Nick seemed to want to drive the point home.

"All right, I get it. No silver. I don't like silver anyway. All my jewelry is gold. Dad insisted." She'd always thought that odd, but her father always got his way, even in such trivial matters.

Come to think of it, they didn't even have silver candlesticks or cutlery. Everything in their household had been gold or gold-plated. Shelly had thought it a bit ostentatious, but that sort of thing was in her father's control, not hers.

When she set up her own home, she couldn't afford to waste money on things like real silverware. Good old steel forks and knives were good enough for her.

Nick's eyebrow arched at her words, but she wouldn't elaborate. Let him think what he liked. Silly arched eyebrow and all.

"So, the silver-bullet-in-the-werewolf thing is true after

all," she spoke her thoughts aloud and had to stifle a laugh. Either she was going nuts or she was starting to believe this whole crazy scenario. Probably both.

"All *weres* share our problems with silver. As do bloodletters and some magic users," Mark confirmed with a straight face. He wasn't joking around.

"Werewolves are real?" she blurted.

"As real as I am, *querida*," Mark confirmed, coming over to her on silent, sure feet. He could stalk in his human form, too, she noted with some alarm. "Wolves, cougars, hawks, predators of many kinds obey the Lords of the Were in North America. My people are from a slightly different part of the world, where older orders of organization apply. We date back to the Mayans, though we were greatly influenced by the influx of Spaniards and those who came later, which is why my friend here sports such exotic coloring for one of our kind." Mark nodded toward the very Arian-looking Nick, who stood on her other side.

She was surrounded by them, and it was intimidating as well as…exhilarating?

She had to get out of there.

"Am I free to go?" She made herself ask the question.

The light in Mark's eyes dimmed as he stepped back. "I will not hold what does not want to be held."

"Come on," Nick said in a gentle tone. "I'll arrange for you to get back to your hotel. I want whoever's watching to think we let you go after questioning and that we believe you to be innocent of any involvement with the gunman."

"I *am* innocent," she felt compelled to put in.

Nick nodded. "My apologies. You are innocent. In so many ways…" He trailed off, gazing at her until she started to fidget.

He turned to escort her out of the room, but Mark stopped her by grabbing her hand. She turned back to look at him and nearly gave in right then and there. But, no. She had to be strong.

"I will arrive at your home tomorrow afternoon. Be ready

18

to give me your answer about working for me then. I will not give up until you agree to at least give me a chance to prove myself to you."

"I'm giving you the chance, Mark," she unbent enough to say. "Just give *me* a chance to get used to all of this. I'm sure I'll have a million questions for you tomorrow. Just give me time, okay? I never expected any of this, and it's a little hard to wrap my head around. Especially after your pal here gave me such a hard time."

Mark smiled. "I promise to give you as much time as I can. And I apologize for Nick, but if you decide to work with us, before long, I believe it will be you giving him the hard time."

Nick grumbled as Mark laughed. She had to get away from him for a while to think, and she had to get while the getting was good…or she feared she'd never leave.

"Are you sure she's safe at the hotel?" Mark asked Nick later that night.

"I've got Heinrich and Mario watching over her. Nothing will get past them." Nick poured another glass of the wine Mark preferred before he uncapped another beer for himself.

"I hope you're right. She is my life, Nick."

Nick took a long swig of his beer before replying. "I'm sorry I was hard on her, but I was too angry about the assassination attempt, and I honestly thought she might have had something to do with it. You know how my temper gets in the way of my other senses. That's why you're the Alpha, Mark."

"Yeah, I have the opposite problem. We complement each other that way. As the Mother of All designed it."

"You have more faith than I do," Nick said ruefully. "I still think our whole system was set up by our predecessors because jaguars are more uncontrollable than other big cat species. We need more checks and balances."

"It's been this way for thousands of years," Mark said for the hundredth time. "We're not going to change it now."

"Did I say I wanted to change it?"

"She is a beauty, isn't she?" Mark observed, raising his glass with a wistful smile on his face.

"Feisty too. You should have seen the way she stood up to me. She was scared, but she didn't cower. For a human, she has some serious guts." He paused for a moment as unease ran through Mark, remembering Shelly was all too human, and therefore, fragile. "I always hoped your mate would be another jaguar, Mark. Are you sure Shelly is strong enough to be Alpha female of our Clan?"

"You yourself said she had guts, my friend," Mark reminded him—and himself as well. "Don't doubt her. The Mother of All would not give our Clan a frail Alpha female." He had to believe that. "She may be human, but many jaguars have taken human women to wife very successfully throughout the ages. It's not that uncommon." And he knew for a fact his words were true. He'd read his people's history. He knew there were plenty of instances where humans bred strong children into the Clan and made terrific mates.

"I hope you're right," was Nick's only reply.

Nick drank the rest of his beer in silence before turning in for the night. They had a big day tomorrow, and Nick had already assigned his best men to watch their unclaimed Alpha female. Her safety had to come before all else. She was the Alpha's—and the Clan's—future...if she gave them the chance.

Everything now—the entire future of the Clan—was up to her.

CHAPTER 3

Shelly woke by slow degrees, stretching in the luxurious bed. The noises of the city below her window eventually clued her in to the fact that she wasn't at home in her quiet suburban house. No, she was in a pricey hotel smack in the middle of midtown Manhattan. Traffic was picking up in the street below as the millions of people who made this city work began their day.

It all came back in a rush. Thoughts of what had happened the night before made her gasp as she remembered the amazing feeling of Mark Pepard's fur—*fur!*—under her fingertips. She'd laid awake most of the night, teetering between believing she must've been the victim of some kind of elaborate hoax and the startling thought that shapeshifters really did exist. Or maybe she was just going mad.

Upset wasn't the word for her state of mind. It didn't even come close. She was in emotional and psychological turmoil. She was questioning all she thought she knew to be real.

Her world had been turned upside down and inside out. And she couldn't even discuss it with anyone. Nick had impressed upon her how dangerous it would be to talk about her discoveries with anyone other than him and Mark on the ride home last night. He'd personally escorted her back to her hotel, riding with her in the back of a chauffeured limousine.

Mark had stayed behind at the old Customs House, leaving by some other route that would take him to wherever he was staying while he was in the city. Only Nick and one of the company drivers accompanied her back to her midtown hotel.

She'd tried to look anywhere but at the disturbing bodyguard. His icy eyes set her off balance, and she'd decided to hate him just about the time he'd threatened to make her *disappear*. Subsequent interaction had made her wonder if maybe she'd judged him too harshly, but it would take a lot to get her to like him. He'd been too mean when he was questioning her, though she guessed he'd had his reasons. Perhaps he really had thought she was some kind of threat to Mark.

It was clear the icy blond bodyguard held his employer in much higher esteem than a mere hired hand would usually have for his boss. This Clan Mark had alluded to sounded more like a family. Perhaps there were bonds that went deeper than mere business connections or even friendships. She had to admit, Nick had seemed almost human there for a few nanoseconds while he'd been talking to Mark. But, of course—if she hadn't been hallucinating—he wasn't exactly *human*, was he? None of them were.

But after Mark had come in and calmed him down, Nick had seemed more reasonable. Maybe he wasn't such a hard-ass, after all. Maybe he just liked scaring the bejeezus out of innocent women for kicks. The jerk.

That thought had helped her ignore him on the ride back to her hotel, for the most part. She kept her anger around her like a shield, but when they neared the hotel, he touched her arm, making her jump. She'd looked at him then, and the way his gaze softened made her almost think he might've regretted being so mean to her before.

Then, he'd gone on to deliver all sorts of dire warnings, admonishing her not to discuss the night's events with anyone. Not even her father. And especially not by phone. He'd made her a little paranoid about possible listening devices too.

He'd said his men had swept her hotel room for bugs when they'd gone in with Mark earlier, but that it was *no guarantee*. Whatever that meant. His people had to keep a low profile, he had gone on to explain, so they could avoid arousing further suspicion around her.

Frankly, she had wanted to scoff at all his cloak-and-dagger warnings, but somehow, she hadn't been able to dismiss them—or his handsome boss—from her mind. Nick's worry about her security, or lack thereof, seemed just genuine enough to make her think twice before discounting it. For now, she would err on the side of caution and follow his advice. Much as it irked her to do so.

There was a great deal to think about before Mark Pepard showed up for their scheduled meeting. *If* Mark had been serious. Many times throughout the night, she had doubted her own sanity. If Mark showed up at her home later this afternoon, she would have to rethink the late-night explanations she had come up with to soothe her troubled mind.

Realizing she had slept late, Shelly got out of bed and headed for the shower. She had to be ready in case she wasn't going crazy. She had to check out, drive home and be ready to confront the jaguar, if he came to call.

*

"You want to remind me why we're doing this again?" Cassius grimaced as he ran his hand down the front of his uniform. That a mighty warrior had been reduced to parading as a bellhop was something his Pack mates would never let him live down, he was sure.

"We're doing it because your big brother promised the Alpha jaguar that he'd help protect the woman. Them jags are scary, man." As usual, his best friend, Gene, summed up the situation with his typical eloquence. "They may be few in number, but they carry a lot of political weight. Not to mention they're wild-ass fighters. I wouldn't want to get on that Nick's bad side. Dude gives me the shivers."

Gene was at least dressed like a normal person, in a designer suit. He was playing floor manager while some of their other male Pack mates were beefing up security and some of the ladies were wearing housekeeping uniforms. But nobody looked as silly as Cassius felt, all done up in gold braid and bright colors. The things he did for the Pack.

"My brother's going to owe me big time," he muttered, hefting yet another piece of luggage onto a cart, helping one of the humans who'd been paid well not to question the influx of new staff.

"Heads up," came a voice in his ear, over the tiny hidden device that connected all the werewolves with the jaguars and other allies they'd pulled in on short notice for this duty. "Activity in the hall outside the lady's room." He knew the voice. It was Ben, one of the tech wizards in the Pack, who'd been sent to the security monitoring room and was watching all the camera feeds.

*

Shelly packed up her stuff and did a quick check around the hotel room to be certain she hadn't left anything behind. She left a tip for the housekeeper on top of the dresser and headed out of her room. Time to face the music.

She was in the hall, pocketing her key when a man came up behind her. He'd appeared from out of nowhere, it seemed, and she gasped as his sudden presence surprised her.

He smiled, but it wasn't a kind expression.

"Forgive me. My name is Antony Mason," he introduced himself, offering his hand. He said his name as if he expected her to know it, but she was drawing a blank.

He seemed polite enough, so she took the offered hand without really thinking about it. She was taken off guard and realized quickly that the hotel hallway was empty, except for the two of them. Nerves began to jangle as she realized just how vulnerable she was at the moment. Sure, there were probably video cameras recording movement in the halls of the hotel, but it wasn't likely anyone would rush to her rescue in time to prevent this man from harming her.

"Pardon my forwardness," he went on, still holding her hand. Something about his touch alarmed her. "I saw you leave last night in a cab with a business associate of mine. He has not returned to the hotel, and I am concerned. Do you know what happened to him?"

She tugged her hand free, using a bit more force than was polite, but it didn't seem to faze him. He just kept that unctuous half-grin on his face, probably trying to pretend he was harmless, when she got a whole other vibe from him. This guy gave her the creeps.

"The man I left with in the cab?" she questioned, stalling for time as she gathered her wits.

He nodded. "The very same. I understood he was on his way to some sort of charity event."

"He was arrested. He had a gun, and I think he tried to shoot someone, though they kept it pretty quiet. Those private security men are very discreet." She decided to stick with the publicly known version of events.

"Aren't they, though?" His half-smile remained as his eyes nearly bore holes into her skull, he was studying her so closely. This guy was not normal. "You say he was armed? I had no idea."

She wasn't buying it. Shelly grabbed the raised handle of her rolling luggage and headed for the elevator. Maybe there would be someone inside the car. She didn't want to be alone with this guy.

"Did they question you about him? You did share a cab with him, after all." His tone was pleasant, but she got the feeling he truly was anything but.

"Of course they did. They thought I knew him, but after a while, they figured out I was telling the truth. We only shared a cab because the bellman put us together. It was raining, and taxis were scarce. We were both going to the same place. It was pure coincidence."

She knew her voice rose in agitation as she rolled her luggage behind her toward the distant elevator. The man who'd introduced himself as Antony Mason followed behind. She was grateful for the couple of feet of buffer provided by the luggage. She got the idea that, if not for the obstacle, he would be breathing down her neck—literally.

*

"Shit. There's a man talking to her," Ben reported to the team of shifters who were monitoring the situation. "He's following her to the elevator, and she doesn't look happy. Jimmy, get in the south elevator now, in case he follows her into the box."

"Roger," came Jimmy's disembodied reply in his ear. Everyone was on edge now. It was show time.

Cassius waited what he thought was a reasonable amount of time, but Ben kept silent. *Everyone* kept silent, keeping the channel clear for orders and advisories.

"Status!" Cassius barked, unwilling to wait.

He wanted to know what was going on, and he wanted to know now. He was in charge of the wolves on this op—by far the largest contingent on scene. If things went south, it was his ass on the line.

"Jimmy's in the elevator with them. The dude followed her right into the box. Doesn't she know better?" Ben's voice in Cassius's ear was both angry and dismayed.

"She's human, Ben. Cut her some slack. They don't have our instincts," Cassius said quickly. "How's it look?"

"Jimmy's behind the male. He's making a face. Something about the guy is off, I think, but we'll have to wait until the box opens before Jim can report," Ben said.

"By that time, we'll have them surrounded," Cassius said with satisfaction. "What floor?"

"She pushed the lobby button. The man didn't countermand her. I've got control of that elevator, and I'm sending it directly to the lobby. No stops in between," Ben reported.

"Good man," Cassius complimented the Pack's tech expert. Ben was a very useful wolf to have around. "Okay, you heard the man. Everybody stationed on the lobby level, converge around the south elevator. Everybody else—I want to know who that guy is. I want his room and belongings searched. Beware possible magical traps. The jags are sideways with a lot of magic users. Be warned."

Cassius was on the move as he issued the orders. He took a full luggage cart and headed for the south elevator. He'd be waiting for the lady when the box opened. And heaven help the stranger if he meant to do her harm.

*

"So, they just let you go? I find that hard to believe."

"Really, Mr. Mason. I'm done with this conversation. Believe me or not. That's what happened." Shelly finally objected to the man's continued questions.

The guy had followed her right into the elevator and kept badgering her. Thank goodness there had been a man already on the elevator when it stopped on her floor. She would not have wanted to be stuck alone with this Mason character.

Of course, the stranger's presence hadn't seemed to stop Mason from cross-examining her. However, she felt like it had stopped him from doing anything more drastic. Thank goodness for small favors.

She'd had enough, though. It was time to go on the offensive. Maybe that would make him back down. It was a tactic she'd used in the past with some success. Maybe it would work now.

"Just who the hell are you, anyway? We've never met before, have we?" She let some of her irritation show as she faced him and deliberately put her luggage between them.

She watched his eyelids lower partially, as if assessing her. He didn't move, but she could feel him take a figurative step back. Her ploy was working—at least a little.

"I'm an investigative journalist. I'm researching a book on Pepard and Balam. I thought maybe you'd have some insider information on what happened last night."

It sounded plausible, but something about this guy gave her the creeps. He wasn't telling her the whole truth. Or maybe none of it was true.

"Well, you're wasting your time. I didn't get within ten feet of Mr. Pepard at the reception, and I have no idea who Balam is."

The first part of her statement was true as far as it went. She hadn't gotten close to Mark at the reception at all. It was *after* that she'd gotten closer to him than she'd ever expected. And she really didn't know who Balam was. The name was as unfamiliar as Antony Mason's.

"Balam is the head of security for Pepard Enterprises." Mason gave out the information as if expecting her to know what he was talking about. He watched her so intensely. As if he was waiting for her to betray some secret knowledge.

"Sorry. Doesn't ring a bell. I did talk to some security people last night, but none of them were named Balam."

Reading Mason's expression was hard, but he seemed to believe her. Thankfully, the elevator pinged, and the doors began to open. The conversation was over as far as she was concerned. She'd weathered the storm and hopefully had passed whatever test this Mason guy had been delivering. With any luck, that would be the end of it.

The door to the elevator opened all the way, and she made a move to get off, but Mason grabbed her arm. He yanked her backward so hard, her arm hurt, and she knew she would be bruised tomorrow. She stumbled but managed to stay on her feet—and as far from Mason as she could manage, which, unfortunately, wasn't far enough.

"If you're lying to me—" Mason hissed near her ear. But he didn't get to finish his threat, because the man who'd been behind them in the elevator put one hand on Mason's shoulder, tugging backward. At the same time, a big man in a bellman's uniform stepped into the open doorway.

"Is there a problem here?" the bellman asked in a deep voice, capturing Shelly's attention.

She looked up at Mason and saw the moment he decided to give in gracefully. He let go of her arm and glanced challengingly at the man behind him then at the bellman in front.

"No problem. I was just helping the lady when she stumbled. Isn't that right, Ms. Howell?"

"No, that's not right." She stepped away, out of the elevator, past the giant bellman, pulling her luggage behind her. "You're a creep, Mr. Mason, and I want nothing to do with you," she added, over her shoulder.

"That's all right, miss. I'll make sure he doesn't give you any more trouble." The bellman gave her a friendly wink as she made good her escape. If anyone could keep Mason away from her, it was the beefy bellman.

"Thank you," she said in a huffy tone, but really, she couldn't help it. She was both scared and irritated, which wasn't a good combination.

Shelly made a beeline for the valet, handing her ticket to the woman behind the desk. She'd called down before she left her room, but she was a little nervous about possibly having to wait for her car to arrive. How long could the bellman really keep Mason at bay?

"Your car is pulling up at the curb now," the lady behind the small desk reported, much to Shelly's surprise.

"That was fast."

"We will delay the man from the elevator as long as possible. Please give the jaguar our best compliments." The woman spoke in a low voice that only Shelly could hear. Nothing showed on the valet woman's face as she took Shelly's ticket and gestured toward her car, which had been driven up to the curb.

A muscular young man was getting out of her driver's seat. He winked at her as he waited for Shelly to join him at the open door. She realized these people were in on Mark's secret. They were probably sent here by him—or Nick—to make sure she got out of here safely. After the encounter with Mason, Shelly was glad for their presence.

"Is the bellman part of your group?" she asked in as quiet a voice as possible.

The lady nodded, smiling. "He is our leader. The silent guy in the elevator with you was also one of ours. Please pass on our vigilance to your Alpha. We are glad to be of help to him."

Relief flooded through Shelly at the thought that what Nick had said last night was true. She was being guarded by Pepard's people in case of repercussions from the night before. She'd resented the idea last night, but after the scary moments with Mason, Shelly was happy to have them around.

"Thank you. I will." Shelly was feeling a little overwhelmed. "Seriously, I can't thank you enough."

The woman smiled at her. "Happy to help." She kept her expression pleasantly bland, but Shelly saw the sparkle in her eye that said more than words. "Now, you best be on your way."

"Right." Shelly straightened her backbone and realized she had to leave. She had to get on the road—away from the momentary safety these people provided. "Thanks again."

Shelly walked over to the car, and the young man took her bag, stowing it in the trunk for her. She handed him a tip, but when she pulled back her hand, he'd replaced the folded dollar bills with a piece of brown paper. A note.

"Thanks. Drive safe now, ma'am," he said, smiling at her as he waited to close her door after she'd sat down.

She'd never gotten such attentive treatment before in her life, even sporting the Howell name. But she couldn't really enjoy it. She faced a long drive ahead of her, and Mason might have friends on the road. She wanted to get home fast. Back to the place she felt safest.

Shelly took off, palming the note until she got to a red light where she could glance down and read the short message.

Drive normally. You have an escort home.

It was signed simply, *Mark*.

Shelly felt her stomach clench in a way that wasn't altogether unpleasant. Far from it.

He had provided for her safety. She'd found Mark Pepard attractive from the moment she laid eyes on him from afar at the dinner, but then, everything had gotten so weird. His people had threatened her. Berated her. Questioned her like she was the bad guy.

There was something about him. Something compelling. Something that wouldn't let her *not* think about him. She didn't know why, but that's just the way it was.

Shelly got out of the city, feeling much better about her drive, knowing there were some folks on the road whose job it was to see she made it home safely. She hadn't really believed the worry Mark had hinted at over possible repercussions from last night, but after that jerk Mason cornered her, and the way he'd tried to grab her when she left the elevator—she was glad of the escort.

It might be ridiculous to think someone would try to harm her on the road, but she'd also thought anyone questioning her about last night had been ridiculous. She'd already been proven very wrong this morning. She didn't want to try for a second round.

CHAPTER 4

"She's safely away," Troy reported in Cassius's earpiece. The lady was in her car and on the road.

That was their cue to release the man from the elevator. With the Pack's help and Jimmy's theatrical skills, they'd managed to delay the guy long enough for the human woman to make her getaway. Cassius had blocked the elevator door while Jimmy lit into the guy with indignant outrage about the way he'd manhandled the lady.

Jimmy was in his element, pretending to be some kind of self-righteous Midwestern preacher, condemning the man and his *big-city ways*. Jim was about to launch into something that Cassius was sure would rival the Sermon on the Mount when they got the all clear. Thank goodness.

"Look, gentlemen," Cassius said in the most docile bellman tone he could cultivate. "Can we just agree to leave pretty young ladies alone and leave it at that?" He made a show of looking around. "I don't want to get anyone in trouble with my boss. He loves calling the cops, and I don't want to do that to anyone." He looked at the creep with a knowing expression. "I'm willing to forget this ever happened." Cassius held out one hand—a clear signal that he'd forget it if the man was willing to grease his palm with a hefty tip.

Personally, Cassius thought that was a masterful touch. No self-respecting bellman would let a guest go without at least trying to milk him for some pocket change.

The man reached into his pocket and pulled out a fat wallet. His gaze seemed to lose some of its suspicion as he forked over a small wad of cash.

Cassius smiled and moved aside for the elevator creep while Jimmy began tsking at him like the outraged preacher character he was playing. He kept it up until the guy left the building. Jimmy left the elevator shortly after, maintaining his persona as Cassius got into the elevator with his luggage cart. They had to maintain the façade in case elevator guy had friends.

As soon as the elevator doors closed, Cassius began relaying orders. "I want that guy followed."

"On it, boss," came the feminine reply. Jilly was on her motorcycle. She'd be great at tracking the lone human through the crowded city streets.

They also had multiple people set up at varying distances from the hotel for just this sort of mission. Jilly would follow for a while then hand off to the next Pack member. They had a big Pack. They could follow the guy for miles and miles.

"Backup team, make him your first priority. We need to know everything we can about him. The jags have a big problem, and we need to give them as much information as possible." Cassius frowned as he thought about what he'd seen when the man was fiddling with his wallet. "What floor was his room on?"

"Eleven," Ben replied over the earpiece. Cassius bent to hit the number and moved upward in the big hotel. He'd thought their job would be over as soon as the lady left, but now, it was looking like it might have only just begun.

"Seal it off, guys. Ben, call Emily and ask her if she can come here right away."

"Emily?" Cassius heard Ben's gulp over the earpiece. Shifters didn't much like magic users, but as witches went, Emily was one of the nicer ones.

33

She did spell work for the Midtown Pack from time to time. And the fact that she was Cassius's aunt didn't hurt. She was loyal to him, if not to the entire Pack. Her sister had been his sire's second wife. Unfortunately, they'd both died together, years ago.

"You heard me. We need her to go over the room," Cassius confirmed.

"Why?" Ben asked. He shouldn't have questioned Cassius, but he let it slide for now. It was rare that any member of the wolf Pack would involve a witch in their affairs, but he knew he had to do it this time. And he knew the rest of the Pack that was in range was listening...waiting for his reply.

"Because that guy had a tattoo on his inner wrist. The one we've been warned about. It glowed with magic," Cassius replied, dread filling his heart at what he had just seen.

"I didn't see any tattoo," Jimmy piped in. Cassius would have to deal with the younger wolf's challenge later.

"You wouldn't. Your magic sense is about as good as your acting." The insult helped Cassius deal with his anger about being questioned. Jimmy was a professional actor. He took a lot of pride in his craft, so belittling it was a grave insult. If they'd been on the street or in the wild, Cassius would have knocked him down a peg or two until he submitted to Cassius's dominance, but the verbal assault would have to do...for now. "Just make the call, Ben. Better yet, send someone to escort her here. Tell her we've got a *Venifucus* situation. That'll bring her."

"*Venifucus?*" Ben gulped again, his voice shaking. He was such a beta.

"That's the tattoo I saw. Elevator Creep was one of them. I want every one of his moves accounted for and in a written report transmitted to my phone hourly. Sooner if he does something suspicious. Understood?"

"Yes, sir," Jilly replied. "So far, he's just sitting in the back of a taxi. They're not going anywhere fast. Stuck in traffic," she replied. "I'll hand off to Luke in another block or two then send you my report."

"Well done, Jilly." Cassius believed in giving praise where it was due among the younger members of the Pack, even if they sometimes questioned him because of his impure lineage. His mother had been a witch. He was only half-wolf, but his wolf was Alpha all the way, and he demanded respect.

In this particular case, though, the magical inheritance from his mother's side of the family had paid off in spades. He'd seen the magical mark when other members of the Pack had been oblivious to it. Forewarned is forearmed, Cassius believed. His being able to spot what the man truly was might have been a fortuitous break.

And in the ongoing battle with the ancient, evil *Venifucus* organization, those on the side of Light could use all the help they could get.

*

Shelly pulled into her driveway an hour or two later. Traffic hadn't been that bad, and she hadn't noticed anyone following her. Then again, she probably wouldn't see them unless there was a problem. That's what Nick had said. And after the scene at the hotel, she believed him.

Problem free, she had made her drive in peace.

She entered her beloved home and turned off the alarm system. Everything here was peaceful and secure, the way she'd left it. The house—one of her own designs—welcomed her as it had for the past several years, and she enjoyed the feeling of security that enveloped her as she kicked off her shoes and sank her toes into the thick carpet of the living room.

She puttered around for about an hour, cleaning areas she had left spotless. She was nervous, expecting Mark at any minute. He hadn't been specific as to what time he intended to show up, and waiting wasn't something she was good at. So, she fidgeted. Trying to work was useless. She ended up doodling and found, after twenty minutes, she'd come up with a stunning likeness of Mark on her sketch pad.

Silly girl. Doodling her latest crush in the margins of her notebook like a lovesick teenager. Shelly laughed at herself as she turned the paper over so that the blank back side faced up. She got up and made herself a cup of tea, deciding to relax as best she could while being on edge, waiting for a multi-billionaire not-quite-human to show up on her doorstep.

At one o'clock sharp, the doorbell chimed. Shelly jumped off the stool in front of her drafting table and took the stairs down two at a time. It had to be Mark. She felt it in her bones.

Sure enough, when she threw open the door, there he was. He was every bit as handsome as she remembered. Perhaps even more so in the crisp light of day. *Damn.*

"Hi." She cursed her breathless whisper.

"Have you eaten lunch yet?" Mark asked, the smile on his face speaking of much more than just lunch plans.

"No." She tried for a firmer tone, but the man stole all her air. That had to be why she sounded breathy and…aroused? *Oh, boy.*

"Excellent." Mark's smile widened. "I took the precaution of bringing something for us to enjoy while we talk. I hope you don't mind."

"Mind?" Why couldn't she seem to speak more than one syllable at a time? She tried again. "No, I don't mind. Thank you." Better. She held the door open and stepped back. "Please come in."

Mark filled the doorway. She tried to get out of his way as he stepped into the house, but he trapped her in his arms, nearly overwhelming her as he propelled her backward. She was almost lifted off her feet by his quick maneuver.

Nick entered the house behind Mark, and then, she heard the door shut and lock.

"Entry's secure." Nick's voice came to her as he passed by on his way farther into the house. Attila the Bodyguard was traipsing around her home like he owned the place, but she couldn't seem to find the wherewithal to object out loud.

She heard the rustling of paper bags right before Mark pinned her against the wall and kissed her senseless. *Good golly, Miss Molly!* The man sure could kiss.

There were no sweet words. No preliminaries. Just possession. Passion. And the pounding of her heart as her blood heated from zero to a hundred and twenty in one second flat.

He lifted her upward, using the wall and his big hard body to keep her in place. She was soft where he was hard, and she began to appreciate just how well they fit together.

The sexiest sounds came from his chest. It was a sort of purring growl, but deep and rumbly, vibrating through her wherever they touched.

Her hands went to his shoulders, encountering the soft leather of his jacket. It was smooth and buttery under her fingers, and it radiated the heat of the man beneath. She wanted it out of the way. She wanted to feel his skin, to run her hands over him and learn his contours and shapes.

She pushed at the leather, and it moved as he shrugged, helping her rid him of the jacket. First, one shoulder, then, the other was relieved of the jacket, and she was able to feel his warmth through the thin fabric of his shirt.

A sound registered, just barely, in the back of Shelly's mind as Mark drew back slightly. She didn't want his lips to leave hers and tried to follow, but he moved out of her reach, leaving her…yearning toward him.

And then, sanity returned.

What the hell *had just happened?*

The loud sound of a throat clearing finally penetrated her fogged brain. She slid away from Mark and moved to put a good five feet between them. Looking around, she saw Attila the Bodyguard eyeing them both with exasperation, his mouth in a tight, grim line.

"Lunch is ready and waiting in the kitchen," Nick said in his gruff voice. "I'll be outside with the rest of the security detail. Try to remember to eat, okay?" He stalked his way back to the front door and let himself out with one last significant look at his boss that Shelly found hard to interpret, though she suspected Nick wasn't happy for some reason.

He probably didn't like her as much as she didn't like him. Fine with her. She didn't have to put up with his bad attitude. If she took the job, she'd be working for Mark, not his rude friend. Right?

She tried to placate herself with that thought as she led the way into the kitchen. She was curious to see what they'd brought. Since Mark was some kind of big cat, did he eat raw meat or something equally repulsive? She wanted to giggle nervously at that thought but kept silent as the wafting scents and aromas finally penetrated her senses.

It smelled like meat, but definitely not raw. No, this smelled more like some kind of roasted chicken with savory herbs. Her mouth started to water as she drew closer to the steaming platters Nick must've laid out for them.

"Wow." She didn't seem to be able to filter her thoughts or words around Mark. She'd have to work on that. She didn't like sounding like a moron.

Mark didn't hesitate. He went right over to the island that separated the kitchen from the dining space. There were comfy stools on the dining room side of the island, and Nick had set the platters of food out on the service side. There was a roasted chicken, as she had suspected, but also a dish of crisp green salad and a selection of vegetables. All gourmet quality and as far from the rubber chicken of last night's event as it was possible to get.

"This looks delicious," she said, just staring at the platters of food. There was a lot there. "I just usually grab a bowl of cereal. This is way more elaborate than I can manage on my own. I'm not much of a cook."

And now, she was babbling. Great. What was it about Mark Pepard that turned her into a ninny?

"I had my chef prepare this for us. She's good with packing things up picnic style, because I move around a lot and eat on the go often. She ends up catering most of my business meals." Mark grabbed a plate—something Nick had also laid out from the bags he'd brought in—and started filling it. "Nick usually insists we bring our own food, since there was an incident a few years back with an attempt at poisoning me. I smelled the poison right off, so there was never any real danger, but Nick does worry that my enemies will find something I can't detect. He says it's safer to just have Marie cook all my meals since she's a trusted member of the Clan. I don't argue because I love her cooking."

The idea of Mark having enemies was real to Shelly after last night's adventure, but it still appalled her to think someone had tried to poison him. That just seemed...low, somehow. It was one thing to come after someone with a knife or a gun, face to face. It was another to poison their food like some sort of ambush. The sneakiness of it disgusted her, but she tried not to let her reaction show as she picked up the second plate Nick had set out.

"I can see why," she answered his statement, firmly not saying the thoughts foremost in her mind this time. "This smells divine."

Mark was everything charming and urbane while they shared the gourmet meal in her kitchen. He complimented the design of the open-concept floor plan she'd devised for this part of her home. He also proved that he'd done his homework overnight and learned more about her past projects and clientele.

Some of the things she'd worked on had been declared private—not for public discussion—by her clients, and Mark even knew about those. His sources for information seemed to be top notch, and he even had photos of some of her more elaborate jobs on his phone. He showed them to her as he referenced architectural points, and she realized he knew a lot more about design than she'd expected.

They could actually have a fairly high-level conversation about the nuts and bolts of her work. He'd asked her about some of the calculations she'd made on certain structures, and she remembered vaguely hearing that he had some kind of engineering background. Apparently, that hadn't just been something to study in college, but rather, it seemed, a passion of his. Huh. The billionaire playboy had hidden depths.

"Everyone I spoke to this morning sang your praises, and after looking more closely at your work and talking it over with you, I can see why," Mark said as the technical side of the conversation wound down. "I admit it was an impulse to ask you to do design work for me last night, but I've learned to trust my instincts, and after a little due diligence, I can see they led me in the right direction once again."

"Then, you were serious about hiring me?" She had thought about it all night long, wondering if maybe the claim hadn't been some kind of ploy.

"I was serious when the offer was made, and I'm even more serious now. I need a series of buildings planned for a new property I recently purchased. It's for the Clan. It will be built by, and for, my people, so their dual nature should be taken into consideration from the very beginning—in the design stage."

"You want me to create a number of buildings with people who can turn into big cats in mind?"

It sounded so ludicrous when she said it out loud, but she could no longer doubt the evidence she'd seen last night. He'd been a cat. A jaguar. *They came from South America, didn't they?* She wasn't sure what they called a person who could turn into a jaguar. She'd never in a million years imagined such a thing could exist in the world she knew.

"Shifters," he told her. "In general, anyone who can go from human to another form—usually an animal form—is called a shifter. Here in North America, and in Western Europe, they're also known as *were*."

"Ah. That explains the term *werewolf*, I guess." She shook her head, barely believing she was having this conversation, but if Mark said it, she was pretty sure it was true. So far, he hadn't lied to her in any way, and he had a reputation for being ruthlessly honest—a rarity among big businessmen.

"I'm Alpha of the Jaguar Clan. Most of my brethren have the tawny spotted coloring you might be familiar with, but

I'm one of the few black jaguars in our Clan. The spots are still there, just hard to see most of the time. Makes me an excellent night stalker." He didn't sound boastful, just stating facts. "Our origins are South America, so we have a slightly different style of government than some of the other big cat shifter species."

"There are others?" she whispered, sipping the excellent wine he'd brought to serve with lunch.

"Many others. The lions have a king. The panthers have a queen they call the Nyx. The tigers have a white tiger as their king, whom they call the Tig'Ra. There are others, but those are the few who are active in this region and are business associates of mine. You might meet them at some point," he added casually, as if her meeting shifter royalty was an everyday occurrence.

"As...Alpha...are you on par with those others who call themselves kings and queens?" she dared to ask.

He shrugged. "Probably. Like I said, we don't use the same style of government as they do. Our lineage and rules of conduct go back to the Mayan culture. The panthers and tigers, at least, only trace their societal organization back to Renaissance Europe. I'm not sure about the lions. They had some catastrophe in Africa that led to an Irish-American off-shoot of the family taking over the whole shebang a few years ago. It's all pretty complicated, and each of us tends to try to keep details of our affairs within our own Clans." He tossed back the rest of the wine in his glass. "But, yeah, I lead all the jaguars. The ones that are left." A sad expression passed over his handsome face. "There used to be a lot more of us, but now..." He sighed and shook his head, dispelling the sorrow that had come to him. "We're rebuilding," he stated firmly, his mood more positive. "Which is why I'm creating a special place just for the Clan. It's what I've been working so hard to build. And I want you to help me make it a reality."

41

CHAPTER 5

Mark reached into the pocket of his jacket and withdrew a folded piece of thick paper. He unfolded it, taking it to the empty dining room table a few feet away and laying it down flat. It was a map of some sort. She moved closer to get a better look.

"It's an island?" she asked, trying to read the complex topographical map for reference points she might recognize.

He smiled at her, but his expression was tight, as if merely thinking about the scope of the project made him tense. His gaze poured over the map, though she could tell from the worn condition of the paper that he must have looked at it many times before.

"I purchased the island some time ago, and I've been waiting...for something." He looked up at her, pinning her with his intense gaze. "I believe now, I was waiting for you."

Of course, there was no way he could have known that he would meet her—an architect of all things—last night, but then again, stranger things had happened. And if the chance meeting had landed her a giant job that would be a pleasure to oversee, then her plan to attend last night's dinner to trawl for clients had worked out for the best.

"What sort of structures did you envision?" Her mind was jumping with ideas. The topography of the island would lend itself to several different schemes. She could see it already in her mind.

"I want a central gathering place. A Clan hall where we can all get together. That would include a communal dining room, kitchen facilities, some kind of ballroom or great hall that could be used for multiple purposes. I'd also want guest quarters attached to the Clan hall itself so that any Clan member who didn't have a permanent dwelling on the island would have a place to stay. A small clinic area to treat anyone who might get injured. We heal fast, but occasionally, we do get hurt bad enough to have to sit it out a few days under someone else's care." He smiled ruefully at that, but she could see he'd put a great deal of thought into this.

He went on to outline more specifics about everything he wanted in that central structure. She was getting a very clear picture of what he envisioned, and ideas were beginning to percolate in her mind. She itched to set pencil to paper to begin sketching out some of her ideas, but that would have to wait until she knew a little more about the scope of the project. She had a feeling he had only just begun.

"I want to take advantage of the wildness of the terrain as much as possible," he went on to say. "We don't want to tear up the jungle. We want to live in it peacefully. Part of it. Like our wilder halves. Which reminds me, you'll have to take our special abilities into consideration in your designs. We're fairly flexible and dexterous, but round door knobs are a no-no." He grinned, and she had to chuckle.

"Let me guess, you prefer the handle or push-bar style," she ventured, earning an amused nod in response.

"Come to the island with me tomorrow and find out," he invited, smiling along with her, though she could tell his invitation was completely serious.

"Uh..." She didn't know him well enough to just go jetting off with him to some private island after only two encounters. Did she?

"We can be there in a few hours. Take off early tomorrow morning. Breakfast on my plane and lunch by the ocean.

Sound good?"

"Um…" She shouldn't agree to go anywhere with this man. Not so soon. Especially not when she knew he could turn into a wild beast at a moment's notice. What if she got to this island of his only to find out she was the main course on the menu for his sharp-toothed Clan?

"Come on," he cajoled. "I guarantee your safety. Scout's honor. And you can have your own guest room for the night. We'll fly back day after tomorrow…unless I can convince you to stay longer?"

She eyed him skeptically. "You were never a scout," she accused gently. "And I thought you said there were no buildings on your island yet."

"I didn't quite say that." He shook his head. "I said I want you to design *new* buildings. There was a mansion of sorts on one side of the island when I bought it. We've been using the existing facilities, including the air strip and the docks, but the area I'm really interested in was considered too rugged by the human billionaire I bought the island from. He stuck to the sandy side where his mistresses could sun themselves on the beach. I'm more interested in the jungle part of the island—which is the majority of the acreage."

"Just how big is this island if it can support its own airport?" She was beginning to realize that Mark Pepard might just be even wealthier than she thought.

"It's not a full-fledged airport. Just a private air strip where we can land any craft in our fleet," he said off-handedly.

"Fleet?" She gulped her wine, not quite used to the kind of society circles Mark ran in.

Oh, she'd been born to wealth, but her father had spent most of their money, and what little remained was tightly guarded. She'd made her own way, her family name gaining her entrée into society circles, but not the highest of the high—which was where people like Mark fit. Her dad had been rich. Mark was mega-rich. A whole different ball game.

Dad had a plane. Mark had a fleet. Dad had a mansion in a good part of town. Mark had his own island with its own air strip and docks. Both rich to most people, but definitely playing in different leagues.

"Many of my people fly. They all have planes. It's not *my* fleet, per se. It's the Clan's," he tried to explain.

But if he was the grand pooh-bah of his Clan, then the fleet was under his direct control, wasn't it? She thought maybe he was playing a semantics game, but she wasn't going to be any ruder than she'd already been. She let it go. There were more important things to think about. His invitation being the main one.

"I'm not sure I should just drop everything to take a vacation in the sun." She tried to wriggle out of it politely, but Mark wasn't giving up.

"It's not a vacation. You'll be working. I'll be putting you through your paces, showing you the rugged side of the island and where I want the Clan hall to be. I can get you most of the way in a four-wheel drive vehicle, but we'll have to do a bit of trekking, as well. I hope you have a good pair of hiking boots. And you'll need whatever supplies and equipment you usually use when doing a site visit. I'll want you to take thorough notes so you'll be prepared to dazzle us with a plan for the Clan hall when you get back."

He was quite the salesman, was Mark. She was already thinking through the motifs and styles she might employ in the kind of project he'd outlined. It sounded like a challenging job, which was her favorite kind. Her fingers were literally itching to grab a pencil and start sketching out rough ideas.

Hmm. She realized she was already doomed. Mark had dangled just the right bait in front of her. Her work was her life, and she enjoyed it. The chance to design something so unique was a once-in-a-lifetime kind of commission. She'd be crazy to turn it down. And she knew already she'd regret it for the rest of her life if she said no.

Despite her fears, she wanted to know more about Mark and his people. The feel of his fur under her fingers was a memory she kept going back to. The remembered tactile sensation went a long way toward convincing her that it was all real when doubt began to creep in. She *hadn't* been dreaming. That memory was so real she could feel her fingers tingle in memory.

The very idea that he'd been hiding this side of himself from the public all these years amazed her. He was often in the public eye, and his least activity was reported in the gossip columns and on the front pages of the society section. His business triumphs—of which there were many—were routinely celebrated on the business television channels, magazines and newspapers.

How had he managed to keep such a big secret when he was under such close scrutiny? There was so much more to his operation—and his people—than met the eye. There had to be. No way could he keep a secret like that without the support of many others.

She couldn't help herself. She wanted to know more about them. She wanted to know more about *him* and how he fit into their secret society. She knew she didn't fully grasp what the term *Alpha* meant. She sensed it was something very important—almost sacred, perhaps. Whatever the case, she wanted to know more. She wanted to understand where he came from and what he meant to his people.

She wanted to see him shift into that amazing big cat again. She wanted to stroke his fur and hear him purr. She wanted…

"So, you'll come?"

The rather loaded question broke into her innermost thoughts. She already knew what her answer would be. She couldn't *not* go. She couldn't give up this opportunity to learn more about him and his people and see them in their natural habitat. Or at least, the place they were actively making their own.

She nodded, still feeling a bit shaky about the decision but willing to commit herself—at least to a visit to the island.

"I'll go, but just overnight. I just need to take some measurements and see the lay of the land in person before I can begin rough sketches." That's all she was going to do there, right?

Yes, she promised herself. That was all. Work. Measure, take notes, observe. That's all. No seducing the sexy boss. No sleeping with him. Not so soon, at least.

She understood the dangerous tenor of her thoughts. She *was* thinking about sleeping with him. And she was acknowledging, at least in her own mind, that she would probably do so after some acceptable period of time had passed.

Oh, boy. She wasn't sure if she was more excited or appalled at her own thoughts.

Mark was enchanted by everything about Shelly. The way she spoke. The way she moved. The bright intellect behind her elegant façade. She was every inch the lady, yet the way he caught her looking at him when she didn't think he was watching made the inner predator in him purr in triumph. She was thinking about pouncing, and he was all for that idea.

Of course, by human standards—the standards Shelly had been raised with—it was way too soon. Shifter culture was a bit more understanding of the needs of the flesh, and there weren't the same stigmas attached to sex as in human culture. Of course, there was also the mate imperative that said, when a shifter was blessed enough to find their one true mate, then they were completely unaffected by any other being.

Single cats liked to roam. That was for sure. But once a feline shifter had found their match, they settled down into a devoted relationship for the rest of their life. It was a dream to strive for. Something everyone wanted to find but wasn't really guaranteed to get.

That Mark had found Shelly—at long last—was a blessing he wasn't about to let get away. He would court her in whatever way she needed. He would give her time to come to him, if necessary, but he wouldn't leave her alone. Never that. No, now that he'd found her, he'd insinuate himself into her life and her work. He'd be always underfoot until, at some point, he won her over completely.

Failure was not an option.

"I'm going to put extra security around your house tonight." He tried to phrase it as diplomatically as possible, but he knew he was being very Alpha with her at the moment.

She'd have to get used to it eventually, because he was the jaguar Alpha, after all. But he was going to try his best to remember she was human and go as slowly as he could. This was a first test to see how she would react.

"Do you think that's really necessary?" She didn't sound pissed, which was a good sign. Her tone indicated a bit of annoyance shaded with concern. Good.

"I always hope for the best but prepare for the worst. I believe you got away clean—except for that little encounter in the elevator—but I've learned it's best not to take chances." And that went double for his mate, though she wasn't quite aware of her special status yet. "Don't worry. You won't see them unless there's a problem. You live far enough back in the woods, and have a large enough property, to easily conceal the people charged with your safety."

"Just how many people are we talking about?" Now, her tone had echoes of challenge. He liked that spirit.

"More than one," he admitted with a grin he hoped would calm her.

"And less than?" she prompted, clearly waiting for his response.

"Less than an army?" he asked, enjoying the banter. She was quick, was his mate. That was good. As a cat, he liked games of any kind, and she was a quick-witted player, which was perfect for him.

"Surely, you can be a little more specific than that." Her gaze danced with lights of amusement, even as she continued to challenge him.

"Less than twenty?" he tried.

She looked appalled. "Twenty? That really is an army."

He gave a long-suffering sigh and pretended to give in. "I

can do ten, if that works better for you, but I don't like it."
He shook his head comically, making a tsk-ing sound.

"I don't see how ten men are going to blend into the little
strip of woodlands surrounding my house. The trees aren't
that dense." Now, she just sounded puzzled.

"Oh, *querida*, you're not seeing the bigger picture. We're
cats. We slink. And we can shapeshift. Not everyone will be
walking on two feet." He smiled as her eyes widened in
surprise.

"Jaguars?" Her voice rose in astonishment. "You intend to
let your people wander round Westchester County as jaguars?
Someone's bound to see one of them and call animal control
or the humane society or PETA, for goodness sake!"

He laughed outright at her increasing concern. "Calm
yourself," he told her gently. "We're professionals. We do this
all the time."

"We?" Her gaze pinned him. "You mean you put yourself
at risk along with your men?"

He suspected the look in her eyes was measuring him in
some way. She didn't seem upset with the idea, more curious.

"I lead from the front," he told her. "As Alpha, I would
never ask any of my people to do something I wasn't willing
to do myself."

"A noble philosophy," she complimented him with a
slight nod of her head. "But seriously, you're not going to be
prowling around outside my house all night, are you?" She
smiled and shook her head. "I don't honestly think I could
sleep knowing you were out there."

He moved closer, seeing an opening he'd be a fool not to
take. "Well, I could always stay inside and protect you up
close and personal." He reached out, stroking her hair away
from her face with the lightest of touches.

He felt satisfaction run through him when she shivered in
response. She was very sensitive to his touch. That would be
utterly delightful to explore in detail…later. First, he had to
get her more used to him.

He didn't honestly think she'd agree to sleep with him on

such short acquaintance. Not his Shelly. Fiercely independent. Stubbornly rigid in some ways, he'd been surprised to discover. And all too human, with human sensibilities about such things.

She was what they called a *good girl*. She didn't sleep around. In fact, the in-depth background check Nick had run on her hadn't found a recent boyfriend in the picture at all. Not for several years.

Something about that both concerned him and made his inner cat want to growl in triumph. She would be his. She just didn't know it yet.

"You could always invite me in," he told her in a low purr that wasn't completely controllable. She affected him deeply.

She laughed. It was a blow to his pride, but a gentle one. She seemed to think he was joking. He wasn't, but she didn't know his moods yet. In time, she would learn. As he would learn all about her. He couldn't wait.

Mark leaned back casually, as if she hadn't just rejected his overture. He'd be a cool cat from here on out, if that's what she needed. He wasn't good at patience, but for her, he'd cultivate some.

"You must think I'm a really cheap date," she went on, oblivious to his inner consternation. "Come to think of it, this isn't even a date. It's a business meeting. I don't usually seal business deals by inviting the client to sleep over."

"That's probably a good policy," he quipped, feeling once more the triumph of knowing his mate was selective. He would have to put some effort into winning her, which pleased his inner cat. "But just in case you're still worried about me prowling around under your window all night, in this particular case, I need to be seen leaving here and going about my business elsewhere. I'm a little too high profile, and after the elevator incident, it's possible you're being watched. If they see me arrive but not leave, that increases their interest in you, which is something I want to control while we can."

She looked as if she was considering his words. She was appropriately serious, but not afraid. That was good. He didn't want her to be afraid of the challenges of a life with him.

"I understand. And I'm impressed at the thought you've put into this. Thank you for being concerned for my safety. I'm not really used to such treatment from my clients."

"*Querida...*" He reached out to take her hand in his. He would be patient, but he also needed to make her aware of his interest in no uncertain terms. "I hope to be much more than a mere client to you."

He brought her hand to his lips and placed a nibbling kiss on the back, moving up to her delicate wrist. She was fine boned, but fierce. His mate was a woman he would enjoy spending years getting to know. Starting right here and right now.

She didn't move back when he moved closer. Her breath caught when he lifted his head and zeroed in on her lips. When his mouth touched hers, she melted into him, as if she'd been waiting all night for this. For him.

Oh, yes. This was the magic of a mate. The perfect alignment of souls. The desire that would never end and always be fulfilled.

Mark kissed like a dream. A fantasy come to life. A warm breath of spring on a long winter's night. Welcome. Refreshing. Utterly enchanting.

But there was a dark side to him, as well. A secret purring beneath his skin. She remembered the feel of the big cat's fur under her fingers and was seduced all over again by the magic of him. Was it her imagination or was something sparking between them?

Mark broke the kiss and moved back to look in her eyes. She didn't want him to go.

"What was that?" he asked, as if he, too, had felt the sparks.

She just shook her head and moved closer. This time, she took his lips, reclaiming what she wanted, taking as well as giving. She would show him that she wasn't just a female to be led around and cajoled into whatever he wanted. She was a strong woman with a mind of her own. Best he knew that at the outset.

She wasn't sure about the truth of it, but Mark had a reputation in the tabloids for being a bit of a chauvinist. She'd nip that right in the bud…if it was true. From everything that she had seen so far, she didn't think there was much truth to that story. Sure, he surrounded himself with big burly security guards, but she'd seen a female face or two at his side, as well.

The press probably mistook the knockout babes who traveled with him as part of his supposed harem, but she'd seen the way he looked at them. As equals. Not as objects. They were part of his Clan, she'd bet. Female shapeshifters with unbelievable power. Strong women whom he respected. It was clear in the way he dealt with them.

Shelly had watched from afar as he'd been about to take the stage at the dinner. Others might have mistaken the woman at his side for his date, but Shelly knew differently. She'd pegged the tall, dark woman as a colleague, not a bed partner. Shelly was seldom wrong about these sorts of things. She'd always had a special sort of radar when it came to judging relationships between people.

She could almost see the bonds that wove between intimate couples. There was a special glow about them that she immediately recognized on some basic level. She'd always known who was spoken for and who was free. Shelly had managed to avoid some messy situations with married men that way in the past, and she trusted her own powers of observation.

Still… It wouldn't hurt anything to double check. She broke the kiss and leaned far enough back to meet his gaze.

"You're not involved with anyone, right?" It was a question, but the way she spoke the words made it more like a statement.

His grin lit his eyes from within. An unearthly light full of magic and wonder. She could get lost in his eyes if she wasn't very careful.

"*Querida*, I would not be here with you if I was pledged in any way to another. You'll learn that I am not that kind of man. The newspapers portray me as some sort of playboy, but the truth is a lot more sedate, I assure you."

She believed him. She might be proven a fool at a later date—though, she thought not—but for now, she trusted her instincts.

"The women in your entourage," she went on, wanting everything out in the open before they went any further. "They're like you. Part of your Clan. Not a harem of girlfriends, like the gossip columns claim."

His eyes narrowed, searching her gaze. "You realized that for yourself, didn't you?"

Shelly shrugged. "I've always been good at reading people and situations."

CHAPTER 6

"You see the truth," he stated it as a fact. A fact that seemed to impress him greatly. He paused, studying her expression for a moment before he went on. "All the people around me are my family. My Clan. I do not have a girlfriend among them. It's been…a while…since my last relationship. I got a little tired of the vapid human women who were all too easy to catch and only interested in what my money could buy them. My beast prefers a more delicate hunt, and as I get older, both parts of my soul would prefer to find a single, true, mate. Someone to share the rest of our life with. Someone my Clan could accept as Alpha female. Someone who could accept them. Love them the way I do. My Clan needs strong leadership. I've managed on my own for a long time, but they need a steadier influence. A mated pair would help the Clan get to the next level. A stability in which to forge families and raise the next generations."

Whoa. She liked that he was being honest with her, but what he was talking about was a little too intense, so soon into their acquaintance.

She put both palms on his chest and pushed back, just the slightest bit. She liked that he immediately moved back, giving her more space, responsive to her desires.

"I can't speak to all that right now, but I'm glad you're

being honest with me. I'll return the favor." He hadn't asked, and she was almost positive his security team had run a detailed background check on her already, but it was only fair to tell him where she stood. It would also give her a chance to catch her breath, both physically and mentally. "I'm single. I haven't been in a relationship in a very long time. I've been disappointed by men a few times in my life, and that has left me somewhat gun shy. So, if you want to start something here…well…you're going to have to bear with me." She looked down at her hands, still resting on his muscular chest, feeling a bit shy now that the bare truth was out there.

One of his hands came up to stroke her cheek. "I can be patient," he whispered, then chuckled. "Not easily, but for you, I can try."

She grinned, looking up to meet his gaze once more. "Well, at least you're honest."

"Honesty," he repeated, pausing slightly. "That is vital between us. It's what I want, always. A firm foundation on which to build."

"You might regret that. I've been told that, sometimes, I'm a little too honest for my own good."

And she had. Her big mouth had gotten her into trouble more than once.

"Never worry about that with me. I read something once that stuck with me. The naked truth is always better than the best-dressed lie," he quoted.

"Who said that?" It sounded familiar, but she wasn't sure where she'd heard that before.

"Ann Landers," he told her, grinning widely. She had to laugh. Big, strong, burly man read advice columns? "My cousin, Nicole, texts me these things, and some of them are actually pretty good."

"Nicole sounds like quite a character," Shelly allowed.

She liked the warmth in his voice when he talked about his relative. She could tell he truly loved this cousin of his, which was somehow reassuring. The heartless playboy the press had painted was nothing of the sort, she was happy to learn.

"She is. But you'll get to meet her tomorrow if you come to the island."

Was he concerned she would back out now, after having given her word? He'd soon learn she was made of sterner stuff than that. Her word was her bond.

"What time do you expect we'll get started in the morning?" she asked, moving away.

The intimate interlude was at an end, and rightly so. She didn't want to end up in bed with this guy on their second encounter. She might be able to stretch and call this a date because he'd brought a meal, but their first encounter had been anything but pleasant in the beginning.

Still. She wasn't the type of woman who fell into bed with a man on their first date. Or pseudo-date. Or whatever this was. Best he realize that now. Though she was having a hard time controlling her impulse to tackle him down to the sofa and have her wicked way with him.

Acting on every impulse was a good way to get into trouble. She knew that from harsh experience.

He allowed her the space she needed and seemed to accept that she was hitting the brakes for now. A true gentleman. Nice.

"Is eight too early?" he asked.

"I wouldn't mind an even earlier start if it means more daylight to scout the building site," she offered.

When he grinned, she knew she'd said the right thing. "How about I send a car for you at six? We can be in the air as soon as you make it to the airport, and hopefully, nobody will discover we're going someplace together. I assume you like your low profile?"

"I enjoy the notoriety my last name garners in some quarters, but you're right. I prefer to stay off the society pages and out of the gossip columns." She reached for her glass, taking a sip as she put even more space between them.

"That may not always be possible when you're with me, but I promise to do everything in my power to keep things quiet as much as I can. In fact, I prefer that myself, believe it or not." He gave her a rueful grin.

"You may prefer it, but the papers seem to follow you wherever you go. Must be hard to live your life in the spotlight like that," she commiserated.

He shrugged. "You get used to it. Up to a point. I let them see as much as will benefit my Clan and keep the rest as quiet as we can. Some of my reputation and supposed exploits is a carefully constructed smokescreen designed to keep the secrets of my Clan. Sort of hiding in plain sight."

She nodded slowly. "I see. That makes a devilishly clever sort of sense."

They talked for an hour or so more until, finally, Nick knocked on the front door with a reminder that Mark probably ought to be seen leaving during daylight hours. Mark shut the door in Nick's face and tugged Shelly into his arms for a long, lingering kiss goodbye.

Her head was still spinning as she watched his car disappear down her long driveway. A slinky shape was outlined briefly in the red glare of the brake lights, and Shelly could swear a feline head turned to stare at her, nodding once before loping off into the trees.

She realized she was clutching one hand to her heart, holding her breath. He'd really left some jaguars on her property to guard her. Sweet stars above! What would the neighbors do if anybody caught a glimpse of the prowlers in the woods—either in human or cat form? She could just see it now—local police with German shepherds and searchlights streaming through the woods looking for intruders. She hoped like hell that the jaguars knew what they were doing.

Then again, they were part of Mark's Clan, and Mark Pepard had a reputation throughout the world for hiring and working with only the best of the best. She knew now that those closest to him were like him. Shapeshifters. Members of his Clan. By all accounts, these shifters were very accomplished people.

That thought firmly in mind, Shelly turned and locked the door. She had a few hours of daylight left and she knew just how she would spend them. Pencil in hand, drawing up lists the old fashioned way. And packing. She was already thinking of what she would need.

But first, she cleaned up what little remained of their lunch. Mark and Nick had taken out the items they'd brought with them, but she'd made coffee using her cups and spoons. She set the dishwasher to run and headed up to her studio to gather a few things she'd need for the trip.

Dawn would come early, and it was time to get ready for what could very well be the biggest adventure of her life.

*

As Mark sat in the back of the black town car, allowing himself to be driven away from Shelly's house by one of his people, he read the encrypted report the wolves had sent through on his phone. Shelly had been hassled by someone on her way out of the hotel. He knew that already from the quick debrief. But the wolves had done a deeper investigation.

His eyebrows rose when he reached the part where Cassius had positively identified a *Venifucus* tattoo on the man's inner wrist. This was not good news.

Mark had known he was a big target for anyone aligned with evil, but to have someone with the might of the secretive *Venifucus* behind him on his trail was troubling, indeed. Mark had no doubt now that the man who had shot at him had merely been a stooge for this other character. For the *Venifucus* would know all about shifter weaknesses and try to exploit them. Hence the silver hollow point bullet filled with pure silver dust.

A bullet designed to take down shifters. A bullet designed to maim and kill with as much agony as possible. For evil fed off such things.

If the *Venifucus* was gunning for him, Mark and his people would have to be extra cautious. Mark forwarded the report to Nick, adding a few comments of his own. He was especially glad now that Shelly had agreed to accompany him to the island tomorrow. She would be out of harm's way once they arrived. Nothing and no one came to the island without the entire Clan knowing about it. She would be safe there.

*

The next morning, Shelly was ready and waiting at six a.m. when the car pulled up. The chauffeur was tall, dark and handsome. Had to be a shifter, Shelly thought as he introduced himself as Mario and showed her an employee I.D. card that said he worked for Pepard Industries as a security consultant.

He was driving a long black limousine with darkened windows. As he took her bags to put in the trunk, Shelly's cell phone rang. She answered, surprised to find it was Mark on the other end.

"Did Mario get there all right?" he asked after a quick greeting.

"He's putting my bags in the trunk right now," she told Mark.

"Good. Can you put him on the line for a moment? I just want to make sure."

Shelly walked over to the car and held out her cell phone. Mark wanted to make sure...of what, exactly? That Mario was who he claimed to be? That didn't sound too safe. If he was an imposter, Shelly would be in a very vulnerable position. Still, she trusted Mark to know what he was doing. Perhaps he would be able to do this in a way that wouldn't put her in any increased danger?

"He wants to talk to you," Shelly said as the driver turned to her. Suddenly, she saw faces in the trees.

Oh, they weren't obvious, but she somehow knew there were shifters watching her every move from just within the trees that bordered her small yard. They were Mark's people. If this driver was a threat, they'd help her. Once again, she trusted her instincts that said the watchers were on her side.

"Alpha?" the man who'd introduced himself as Mario spoke into the phone. Shelly relaxed marginally. He'd called Mark by the shifter title. The Jaguar Clan Alpha. Would a bad guy know to do that? Probably not. She hoped.

After a few words, Mario handed the phone back to her with a sheepish grin. "It's okay. He was just checking," Mario told her, rather vaguely, then went about closing up the trunk and headed around to the passenger compartment to open her door while she got back on the line with Mark.

"Um... Okay?" she asked him, not sure how to phrase her concern in a way that wouldn't sound like it. It was too early to be playing word games.

"Yeah, Mario's good. He'll get you to the helo pad. You can get in the car. And don't be concerned if you see a few other cars following or ahead of you. The security team is going to leave a small presence at your house, to make sure nobody tampers with it while you're gone, but the rest are going to be escorting you to the plane. A blond guy named Heinrich will be your chopper pilot. He'll be in one of the security cars."

"I'm taking a helicopter to the airport?" That was news to her. And kind of exciting. She'd never been in a helicopter before.

"It's the quickest way. Is that all right?" he asked, almost as if he was unsure of his strategy.

"Yeah, it's fine." She tried to sound as if she flew in helicopters all the time but probably wasn't very convincing.

A wry chuckle sounded at the other end of the line as she got into the limo. "Next time, I'll be sure to run my plans past you before I spring them on you. Sorry for the surprise. I'm not used to consulting anyone else, but I'll get better. Promise."

Why he'd want to get used to consulting her on his plans was something she didn't quite want to contemplate at the moment. He sounded so serious about her, but she was still getting used to the idea. It would take time for her to catch up to him.

That was new. Always before, in the few disappointing relationships she'd had to date, it had been her unrealistic expectations that had gotten her into trouble. Or—maybe her expectations hadn't been all that unrealistic. Maybe the men she'd been expecting things from just hadn't been quality candidates for the position of husband and life mate.

She'd been way more committed than any of her past boyfriends. As she'd told Mark last night, that had made her more than a little gun shy. She was hesitant to commit her feelings to anyone now. She'd been burned once too often.

In a huge switcharoo, Mark was the one who seemed to want to rush into full-blown future planning. She was on the other side of the equation this time, and it felt damned odd.

Mario was driving down the road as she finished the call with Mark, with a promise to see him soon. He'd be waiting, he'd told her. A shiver went down her spine at the thought of seeing him again.

This would be their third encounter. Possibly their second date, if being whisked away to a private island constituted a date. She thought it probably did.

Was it still too soon to consider sleeping with him? She hoped not. She was quickly running out of excuses. Her instincts said to grab the brass ring while it was close enough to touch. The future was uncertain. She should probably enjoy the time she had with this amazing man while she could.

As she daydreamed about what might happen on the plane, or when they got to the island, she noticed the cars he'd mentioned, following behind. There was one in front, as well. She probably wouldn't have spotted them if Mark hadn't told her about them, but since she knew what to look for, it was pretty clear she had an escort.

When they reached a private heliport, she noticed that a total of three cars, including the limo she was in, drove straight out to a hangar in the distance. At least one other car stayed near the entrance, possibly to run interference.

Her limo drove right up to a helicopter that was attended

by two tall, good-looking people—a male and a female, who nodded to Mario and helped move Shelly's luggage from the trunk of the car to the back of the chopper. A handsome blond man went straight from one of the other vehicles to the helicopter and started checking things over in a confident way. The woman who'd been standing ready with the chopper conferred with him as they discussed points on a clipboard she held.

When Shelly's bags were safely stowed, Mario took his leave of her and drove the limo back the way they'd come. She was escorted into the helicopter by the man who'd helped Mario with the bags. He made sure she was securely buckled in and gave a headset, plus a little basic instruction on how it worked. Then he left, going back into the open hangar behind the helicopter.

By the time all that was done, the blond man was in the pilot's seat, the woman beside him. Both had donned headsets as they began to power up the machine. Shelly didn't want to interrupt them, though she found she could switch channels on her headset and listen in on their discussion of the pre-flight checks.

It was typical pilot jargon that she only half-understood, but it was reassuring, in its way, to listen to them talk so casually. They obviously knew their stuff and were experienced pilots. When they finished, the blond man turned in his seat to look back at her. The passenger compartment was big enough to seat four comfortably, but Shelly had it all to herself.

"I'm Heinrich," the pilot said over the headset. "This is Lucinda." He gestured toward the woman in the copilot's position. "Are you comfortable back there?"

Shelly gave him a thumbs up, as well as verbal confirmation. "I'm ready when you are. And I'm Shelly, by the way. It's nice to meet you both, and thanks for the lift."

Both of them smiled back at her, but it was Heinrich who spoke. "Happy to help. Sit back and enjoy the ride. It's just a quick hop to the airstrip. Shouldn't take more than ten or fifteen minutes."

Shelly nodded as the pilots turned back to their instruments and the blades began to turn in earnest. Within moments, they were flying.

A near-vertical takeoff was new to Shelly and something to marvel at. As was the scenery below them. She recognized the streets around her home as they turned toward the west, and then they were out, past her house, and headed for a nearby regional airport. They were flying much lower than airplanes flew, and the sky was clear, so the views were spectacular.

Almost too soon, they were coming in for a landing next to a private hangar that was some distance from all the others. Shelly saw a small jet waiting there and had to admire the shiny white vehicle. She didn't know all that much about jets, but she recognized the quality of the vehicle and the fact that it was close to brand new. Only the best for the billionaire playboy who also happened to be the secret leader of a band of highly magical shapeshifters.

For a moment, Shelly wondered if she was hallucinating this whole situation, but then, she looked at Heinrich and Lucinda—two impossibly good-looking and lithe beings— and realized they were shifters. Probably golden jaguars with spots. Slinky. Sleek. And intensely powerful.

And Mark was their leader.

Faced with the proof of them right there in the helicopter with her, she had to admit, this was probably real and not a dream. She waited for Heinrich's signal that it was safe to unbuckle her seatbelt and then let the impossibly handsome and muscular ground crew open the door and let her know it was safe to come out.

She was escorted to the waiting plane without any delay, and she saw someone following with her bags. She felt a bit like royalty, the way they were seeing to her every need. As she mounted the steps up into the small jet, she noted Heinrich following close behind. He veered left into the cockpit as she was ushered into the body of the plane, where

Mark was already seated, waiting for her.

He got up to greet her with a kiss on the cheek, and she blushed as she became aware of Mark's people watching them very closely. Lucinda had also come aboard and was heading into the cockpit behind Heinrich. Through the open door, Shelly spotted another man already in the pilot's seat, flipping buttons and talking into a headset.

When the cockpit door closed, only Mark and Shelly were left in the cabin for a moment. Shelly had seen her bags being stowed in a closet near the door by the man who had brought them up into the jet. Then, he'd left again with a quick nod to Mark.

"Was the chopper flight okay?" Mark asked as he motioned for Shelly to pick a seat from the choices available.

The jet was laid out like someone's living room, not like a commercial airliner. Instead of rows of seats, there was a conversation area with a couch and coffee table. There were also a few seats that looked like they had workstations built in for those who might want to set up a temporary office while they flew from one place to another.

Mark had been seated in one of the comfy-looking chairs, so she chose the one next to him. She'd try it out. They could always move later, she supposed, if they wanted to.

"I've never flown in a helicopter before. It was seriously cool," she admitted, grinning at him.

"I'll have to take you up more often," he said, smiling in what looked like approval. "We'd better buckle in for takeoff. The sooner we get off the ground, the sooner we get to the island. I can't wait to show it to you."

He sat in his seat, next to hers. They took a moment to buckle in, and when Shelly looked up, she realized they'd been joined by a few more people. There was an older woman with a kind face, a younger woman who looked enough like her to be her daughter, two very large men who could have been twins, and Nick. They were all buckling into seats farther up the cabin, closer to the cockpit.

"I'll introduce you once we're underway," Mark told her

quietly as the jet started taxiing toward the end of the runway. He surprised her by taking her hand in his. Their chairs were close enough that her left armrest brushed against his right. He lifted her left hand to rest between them, entwining his fingers with hers. "I missed you."

His softly voiced words rang true in her mind, and she realized she'd missed him too. Odd as it seemed. She'd almost been counting the hours between the moment he'd left her last night and this morning when she'd see him again. She couldn't remember ever being this eager to see a man— even when she'd been a hormonal, daydreaming teen. Only Mark elicited her stalker-ish tendencies.

The flight passed in a bit of a blur. Mark introduced the team once they were airborne, but the others kept a respectful distance for the most part. The older lady proved to be Marie, Mark's personal chef, and the younger woman was, indeed, her daughter, Janice. They produced an array of breakfast foods they had packed to share among them all. Shelly noted that they brought trays up to the cockpit, as well.

There was no real demarcation between Mark and his people. Sure, they all treated him with respect, but he treated them the same way. As if he valued each and every one of them. Like they were family, not mere servants. Shelly liked that.

For the most part, she sat and talked with Mark about his visions for the type of community he wanted her to design on the island. He described some of the terrain and showed her a smaller version of that topographical map at one point, but she knew the reality of the place, when she saw it, would spark her imagination.

Although…some of the motifs Mark was describing were already causing creative thoughts to flow. He'd brought along a portfolio of inspirational images. Everything from penthouse apartments to ancient ruins in South America. The jaguar motif was something he wanted to feature, not hide, and she thought of ways to include the cat's attributes into her buildings.

There would be the obvious artistic representations, of course, but she also thought about doing something subtler. Like using the sinuous tail of the cat as a model for the curved façade of one of the larger buildings. It would be like nothing she had ever designed before. It would be unique. Magical. Challenging.

She was looking forward to getting started.

By the time the jet landed, Shelly was ready for her adventure to begin. She peered out the window of the plane eagerly, not surprised to find a lush green landscape waiting for her. It looked like a tropical paradise. She could also see the classically-styled mansion set on top of a nearby hill.

"That's the original owner's house. We use it as a base of operations now. After the new community is built, the mansion will serve as a buffer between our Clan home and the outside world," Mark told her as the jet taxied toward a distant hangar. "We don't get a lot of outside traffic here, but there is some, and we do have to maintain the human fiction for the rest of the world. As far as anyone outside the Clan knows, I'm going to live in that monstrosity over there, and you're here to design unobtrusive staff housing." He shrugged. "We might even build a bit of it in plain sight near the mansion, in case anyone is watching via satellite, but the real work will be under cover of the jungle canopy, where eye-in-the-sky can't see too well."

It was an ingenious plan. He'd hide his new community in the jungle where few, if any, would ever even suspect it. She already knew all the building would be done by his Clan members. They'd probably also be the ones bringing in the supplies. It would be next to impossible for anyone outside his Clan to keep track of what they were building here. The plan was nearly perfect.

CHAPTER 7

The air was moist and humid, but not unpleasant, when Shelly walked down the steps of the private jet. The scent of tropical flowers was in the air, along with moist, loamy earth, delicious to her senses.

She noted a large docking facility for boats not too far away, along with a very utilitarian warehouse near it. That was where the supplies came in and were stored, she realized. In fact, a large boat was moored there right now, with a few bare-chested men toting boxes back and forth. An efficient-looking woman with a clipboard was overseeing the whole operation.

Shelly waited on the tarmac for Mark. She'd seen one of the men from the cabin take her bags down already, and she gave up worrying about where they'd end up. Mark's people were competent and well-organized. She'd probably find them waiting for her when she arrived at her room for the night.

The only thing she'd kept back was her drawing case. She'd asked Mark about it during the flight, and Nick had been able to easily retrieve the small portfolio that contained the tools of her trade, which included a laser measuring device, as well as a good old-fashioned tape measure, just in case. She also had pencils, plenty of paper and a fully charged tablet computer that she might need, depending on what she found when she got to the building site.

"What do you think?" Mark asked, coming up beside her.

"It's beautiful. Although, I might clad that warehouse in something a little less reflective, which would cut down on the glare off the roof. There are a few materials available now that are both protective and insulating that might do the trick."

"We went with that skin to keep the temperatures inside within reason," Lucinda said, coming up beside her. The woman moved so silently—all of the jaguars did—that Shelly had to try hard not to jump at her sudden appearance.

"Yeah, I can see that. It's a good way to go, but there are newer materials out there that could do the same and be less of an eyesore. I bet that roof shines over at the house when the angle of the sun is just right," Shelly commented, judging the distance from house to warehouse and the position of the sun.

Lucinda laughed. "Yeah, that was an unexpected side effect when we built the warehouse, but we got used to pulling the shades or just not going into those rooms at certain hours."

"You were involved with the warehouse project?" Shelly asked, since the female pilot seemed knowledgeable on the topic.

"My little brother designed and built the thing," Lucinda said proudly. "He's not formally trained, but he's got a bit of talent for construction. He got the plans from one of his contacts in the Redstone Clan.

Now that was a familiar name. "Redstone Construction? They're one of the best companies out there," Shelly agreed. "But why do you call them a Clan?" Shelly wondered at the implications. "They're not... They..." She turned to look at Mark, who was just standing there, looking amused. "Are they jaguars too?"

"Cats," Mark replied. "But not jaguars." He paused, and she absorbed the meaning of his words. Holy crap. There were shifters everywhere!

"Cats? Like housecats? Or like lions?" she squeaked.

Both Lucinda and Mark laughed as the three of them started walking toward the path that led to the mansion. It would be a bit of a hike to the building, but Shelly needed the exercise after being cooped up for the past few hours.

"Cougars," Lucinda finally replied. "The Redstone family are all cougars, but their Clan is a very inclusive one. Basically, any shifter group that wants to work for the construction company agrees to come under the leadership of the Redstone Alpha, so Grif Redstone has all sorts of shifters under his banner. Wolves make up a large part of the construction crews, but there are bears, other cats, raptors and who knows what all working for Redstone in one capacity or another."

"Raptors? You mean like birds of prey?" The only other thing that word brought to mind was the scary velociraptors from that old movie franchise, but Shelly didn't think there was such a thing as a dinosaur shifter. Was there?

Lucinda was nodding. "Hawks, eagles. That sort of thing. They make natural born iron workers since heights aren't really an issue for them."

"Wow." Shelly didn't realize she'd said that aloud until Lucinda chuckled. Well, she probably already looked foolish, so she decided to ask the question still lingering in her mind. "Are there such things as dinosaur shifters?"

Mark guffawed but then seemed to control his amusement. "Sorry. As far as I know, the dinosaurs really are extinct, though I did hear a rumor that there were once dragon shifters. Of course, I've never seen one, or know anybody who has. I think, if they ever did really exist, they probably died off in the Middle Ages when knights were actively hunting them."

"I'll see you up at the house," Lucinda said before taking her leave off a side path that connected with the one they were on.

Lucinda was gone before Shelly even had a chance to raise

her hand in farewell, her mind was still stuck on the idea of dragon shifters. Though her responses were probably a bit sluggish from all the travel. These jaguars were quick. Shelly would have to up her game if she was going to keep up with them.

She assumed the path Lucinda had taken would lead to the warehouse. She'd practically disappeared into the jungle foliage. Even here, where it was carefully manicured and held at bay along the pathways, the leaves were thick, though Shelly noted someone had already felled any of the larger, old-growth trees in this immediate area. It had probably been done when the mansion was built by the previous owner.

"We already have a skeleton crew living on the island. Most are housed in the mansion, but a few like to live a bit wilder, so don't be surprised if you run across a few folks like that." Mark nodded his head toward the curve in the path ahead of them, where Shelly was surprised to see an absolutely gigantic jaguar sitting in the shade of a huge fern.

The cat stirred itself as they approached, sitting up and nodding to Mark as they passed. Shelly felt her heartbeat accelerate. The cat was massive, and she had no doubts those sharp teeth could rip her to shreds. She just had to remember there was a human mind in there, along with the cat's. It wouldn't attack her without provocations, right?

"You maintain your intellect while you're shifted, right?" she asked, realizing she should have clarified some of this before she had agreed to come to Mark's private island.

He put his arm around her shoulders and tugged her close. She went, enjoying the protective feel of his warmth. "We do. None of my people will harm you, Shelly. You are our honored guest. And on this island, the only big cats you see will be my people. Nobody will hassle you, even if you're out here alone. I promise."

Reassured by his words, she was still a little leery when they came upon another spotted cat lazing in the shade around another bend in the path. This one was much smaller, and Mark stopped to bend down and gently stroke the youngster's head with clear affection.

"Where's your mama, huh, Kensi?" he asked as the cub, who made a mewling sound and turned her head up the path toward the mansion. "I bet she's looking for you," Mark said, standing up with the furry little jaguar in his arms. "Why don't we go back and see if Marie has any cookies for you?"

At mention of the treat, the little cat hugged Mark's neck, settling into his embrace as naturally as a human baby might cuddle. Shelly couldn't help but feel a tugging on her heart strings as she watched the big man carry the little cub the rest of the way to the house.

Mark was good with kids. The proof was in the way the little cub had curled so trustingly into his arms. This baby knew him and knew she could trust him. Children had an instinct for such things, in Shelly's experience.

"This is Kensi, and she's five years old," Mark told Shelly as they continued the walk toward the mansion.

The path sloped upward at a gentle climb, but Shelly was feeling it in her calves. She wasn't in as good shape as she'd thought, but Mark handled the trek and the extra burden of the child with ease. In addition to being beautiful in both human and animal form, jaguar shifters apparently had a lot more stamina than human architects.

"Kensi's mom and dad are on paper as the housekeeper and head groundskeeper of the estate, but that's just for the IRS. Kensi's parents are both healers, and they look after the Clan when we need patching up. Ah, there's Jim now."

Kensi perked up and tried to launch herself out of Mark's arms toward the man who was coming down the path toward them.

"You found her," Jim said, taking his daughter into his arms. "She was pestering Judy to take her down to the airstrip to meet your plane, but then she disappeared, and I figured that's where she'd gone. How far did she get?"

"Just about halfway," Mark said and Shelly thought she detected a hint of pride in his tone. "She's going to be a strong jaguar someday," he went on to praise the child, who was clinging to her father but looking back at Mark with adoring eyes.

She really was impossibly cute. Shelly felt her heart fill with…something. Some pang of longing she'd never really experienced before. Kids had never affected her much. They were cute and all, but babies never seemed to fascinate her the way they did some of her friends.

Now, seeing Kensi, adorable in her spotted cat form, Shelly began to get an idea what that maternal instinct was all about. Somehow, this little cat-child was striking a potent chord in Shelly's being.

Huh. Maybe she'd just never seen the *right* child before. Maybe something deep inside her—that instinct that she trusted so much in all other aspects of her life—knew that a human child wasn't the thing for her. No. Maybe a *shifter* child was what was meant to be…

"Shelly, this is Jim, Kensi's father and my first cousin." Mark introduced them.

"Hi," Shelly said. "Your daughter is beautiful," she complimented, realizing the little cat's eyes were now focused on her.

"She's a handful," Jim agreed, as they all began walking back toward the house. "She's at that age where she wants to assert more independence, but it's really not good to worry your mama," Jim finished, directing his words to the little girl and kissing the top of her head.

The little cat made a mewling sound that melted Shelly's heart.

Mark watched Shelly's reaction to Kensi with particular interest. She didn't seem repulsed by the idea that the little cat was actually a little girl, as well. That boded well for his future plans. If all went as he hoped it would, someday, Shelly would have a child of theirs who might be able to transform like Kensi. It was important that Shelly not be too shocked by the idea of shapeshifter children.

They ate lunch at the mansion with a number of Mark's

Clan mates. Everyone was on their best behavior, much to his amusement. They were both wary of making him look bad to the only human woman he'd ever brought to meet his Clan, and curious as only cats could be about her. The conversation was casual, but every once in a while, someone would ask a question that was a little too direct.

Shelly handled it well, though Mark was a bit embarrassed by some of the questions that she fielded. The one about her family's fall in fortune was particularly awkward, but Shelly didn't seem to mind. At least, she gave no outward sign that the prying questions were at all out of the ordinary.

When the inquisition masquerading as lunch was finally over, Mark showed Shelly to a guest room where her luggage had already been placed. His room wasn't far away, and if he had anything to say about it, Shelly would be sleeping with him tonight, but for the moment, he'd give her a few minutes to freshen up and prepare for the afternoon's trek deeper into the jungle.

He left her at her door with a peck on the cheek. He wanted more, but he had decided on a strategy and was sticking to it. She was in his domain now. He had time and space in which to work his plan…and hopefully create a little magic.

Mark met with his staff for the twenty minutes he'd allotted, getting updates on critical business situations and happenings on the island while he'd been away. His people were more than competent, and he was able to delegate much of his work for the next day or two. He'd have time to court Shelly.

Everyone in the Clan knew that when a jaguar scented his mate, everything else became secondary—at least for a while. Once the mating was solid, other things might recapture his attention somewhat, but the mate was paramount. Once found, a mate would change a jaguar's life forevermore.

And in Mark's case, his mating would impact the entire Clan. Shelly could be the instrument of change for everyone on this island and all the jaguars he intended to bring here. To bring home.

Because he wasn't just building some kind of resort community for jaguar shifters here. No. Mark's plan was to build a place where they could all live together. Protected. Isolated when they wished to be. A jaguar sanctuary.

It was time to call all his people home and rebuild the Clan.

*

The trip out to the building site wasn't as rugged as it had been the last time Mark had done it. While he'd been in the human world, his people had been busy pre-positioning huge stacks of basic building materials that would be needed once construction began. They had to be cautious, bringing in small shipments to the warehouse a little at a time, so as not to draw notice from the humans on shore.

Getting the stuff to the building site required that they widen the jungle track they had carved out of the foliage. Careful to leave the sheltering trees in place so their temporary road would be hard to discover from above, they had nevertheless created a more passable pathway under the cover of the leaves. It was almost like a green tunnel in places, and Mark watched Shelly look around in wonder. He liked her reaction.

"I can't believe what you've done here," she remarked as the four-wheel drive vehicle bumped along the trail. "This is like something out of a movie."

"It's been greatly expanded since I was here last," Mark admitted.

He was driving, and it was just the two of them in the Jeep. He had wanted time alone with her. He'd also wanted to see her reaction to the spot he had chosen for the future home of the jaguar Clan. Maybe it was selfish of him to want to keep her all to himself for now. Or, judging by the cross examination she had suffered at lunch, maybe it was the smart thing to do.

"They're really gearing up to build as soon as we have a solid plan for the structures. In the meantime, we've been stockpiling supplies and prepping the area as best we can," he told her as they came over a rise in the landscape.

They had been steadily climbing since they left the mansion. The spot he'd chosen to build on was at a high point on the island, but there were taller peaks around them still. The idea was that they'd be sheltered on three sides by the rocky terrain, leaving only a small area through which they could see the ocean—or anyone on the ocean could possibly see them.

If they built the right kinds of buildings, nobody would be able to detect them from the sea or satellite. Their new home would be as secure as Mark could make it, while still allowing the freedom and beauty of their location to shine through.

He stopped the Jeep atop the final ridge to give her a good view of his chosen location. Her reaction didn't disappoint. Particularly since the guys had been busy prepping the area. It wasn't clear-cut by any stretch of the imagination, but what they'd removed so far helped the natural contours of the land be more visible—at least from this angle.

"Oh, wow," she breathed, her focus strictly on the landscape. Her mouth hung open a tiny bit in what looked like awe.

Mmm. He liked that. In fact, he wanted to kiss her so badly in that moment, he had to grab the steering wheel so tightly he almost ruined it.

Get a grip, amigo. He didn't want to scare her off. He had to let her get used to him before he pounced too enthusiastically, but she wasn't making it easy. She was just too damned attractive—which was a good thing overall, but right now, it didn't help him be the gentleman he was trying so hard to be.

"Is this a caldera?" Her expression changed as she turned to him, a little frown between her eyebrows that he found utterly adorable.

Damn. His lady was smart. The cat in him purred in

approval.

"The entire island is an ancient volcano, yes," he told her. "This is the place where the lava flowed, but it's safe now."

"How can you be so sure? I mean, the Atlantic isn't as active as the Ring of Fire in the Pacific, but things can change. If you're planning long-term, this might not be the best place…" Her gaze roamed back to the landscape before them as if it called to her.

"It *is* the best place. I'm not sure how much you know about South American traditions—myths and legends—but the jaguar holds a special place in the ancient lore of many areas for a reason. We are close to the earth. We are part of it. My people have a sense of the danger spots, and this isn't one of them. The lava that flowed to create this island is long gone and will not return to this spot. I feel it in my bones. It's as if this place was made for us. To shelter us and give us a chance to start over." He, too, was looking out at the valley created by a long-ago volcano, surrounded by tall, curving peaks that would hide them so perfectly.

"Start over?" She turned back to him, concern in her expression.

Mark sighed. It was time to come clean. "My people have been in decline for a long time. We were hunted. Families were scattered due to wars and migration. The drug trade has been particularly hard on us, since many of my people were local leaders or shaman and tried to stand against the cartels. Most were slaughtered as they tried to protect the humans in their areas. We have a lot of orphans."

"That's terrible," she breathed, compassion clear in her voice.

"That's why I work so hard in the anti-drug area, and the cartels know I am their enemy. They don't dare come near me anymore, but they've spread their poison far and wide. I'm only one man, and though my organization is strong enough to stand on its own, we cannot take on all the drug lords by ourselves. Not now." His face tightened as resolve to work his plan filled him once again. "I'm thinking long-term.

If the jaguar nation can rebuild and become a strong unit—like we have never really been before—we might have a chance at doing something really worthwhile for the entire world. But that time is not now."

"You have to regroup first," she whispered. "You have to come together and rebuild the family and the Clan into something so strong, it can never be decimated again."

He looked at her with renewed respect. She understood. His mate was a perceptive woman with a big heart. The jaguar had chosen well.

"Exactly. And this is the place we will do that. In times past, we were strong individually because the enemies we fought were localized and we had jaguar magic on our side. We lived in discreet territories. Each family had their own claim to defend and protect. We got along for the most part, but our cats liked to spread out."

"How is grouping you all together here in one place going to work out if your cats like to have their own space?" she asked, getting the gist of his challenges quickly.

"Well, for one thing, we have a big island to roam, and we've all agreed to specific rules about which parts of it belong to which family group. We'll respect each other's boundaries in the jungle, and we're used to living as humans in a community. The settlement we build here will be big enough for us to each have our own territory, but close-knit enough that we're all here for each other—to raise the orphans and give them a sense of family. To care for the few elders who are left. To have families and grow strong again—this time as a unified group." He felt the steel of his conviction down to his toes. "And we'll rip apart anyone who tries to stop us. This place has only one way in or out if you're on two legs. It can be easily defended. And if the worst should happen and we need to flee, we go in cat form where humans cannot follow."

"You've given this a great deal of thought," Shelly said, respect in her voice.

"I've had decades to think about this. I shopped around

for just the right location and finally convinced the former owner of this island to sell. He was getting too old to enjoy it properly, anyway, which made the sale easier. And I gave him visitation rights to the mansion for as long as he lives. He's a good guy, for a human."

"You old softy," she said, surprising him with her teasing tone.

He chuckled. "Don't let anyone hear you say that. I have a certain reputation to maintain."

Her laughter enchanted him. Low and intimate. A joke shared just between them. It had been a long time since he'd had anyone to confide in. Anyone to joke with. Anyone who didn't automatically defer to him because he was the Alpha cat. He hadn't really realized it until this moment, but there was truth in that old adage: It was lonely at the top.

If he could convince Shelly to be his mate, then he'd never be lonely again. She would be his counterpart, his confidant, his lover and his companion…as he would be hers. He'd heard humans wanted such things in their lives, as well. He knew there were billions of love songs and romantic books and movies out there that gave credence to that idea. Maybe it wouldn't be so hard to convince her to be his, and his alone, for the rest of their lives.

CHAPTER 8

They spent the rest of the afternoon touring the site on foot and, where possible, in the Jeep. Mark introduced Shelly to various members of his Clan who were busy clearing space in a very deliberate way so as to keep the canopy of leaves above them intact while making it possible to move freely below and have room to build.

This would be a unique project in that Shelly would have to consider the coverage from above and work much more with existing trees and landscape than usual. She liked the challenge, and ideas blossomed in her mind as she saw each new part of the cleared area. Perhaps there was a way to incorporate some of the larger trees right into the buildings. She'd have to look into how that might work long-term, but she would definitely like to try that in a few places.

The first of the buildings to go up would be a sort of community center they referred to as the Clan home or Clan hall. Not only would it be a place for communal gatherings, but there would be a sort of hotel component with individual suites of rooms for Clan members in need of temporary housing.

"We'll eventually have several communal buildings, each devoted to different purposes. I envision a school for the children, a training center for martial arts for young and old alike, places where different interest groups could gather to teach and learn various crafts, and each building would have a natural component, incorporating the beauty of our natural surroundings so that Clan members could participate in either of their forms." Mark was waxing eloquent on his ideas and plans for the space. Shelly just listened, taking it all in, beginning to understand his vision for each area they surveyed. Shelly was taking meticulous measurements and making lots of notes.

Mark had big plans. There was no doubt left in her mind about that. But this was a place of epic beauty and ominous beginnings. She'd never been asked to work in the caldera of a dormant volcano before. She doubted she would ever get this kind of chance again.

She felt almost as if she was building some super villain's secret lair. It was like something out of a movie—or a comic book. It was so over the top, it was almost funny, but at the same time, she could feel the texture of the earth beneath her feet. She could see the intense life in the greenery all around her. She could even detect the glimmer of obsidian in the few exposed rock faces. Volcanic glass. Black as Mark's fur and said to have magical properties.

This was a special place. She could feel it in her bones. That instinct she'd never been able to put the proper name to tingled. It told her that this was the right place. A good place. A place where Mark and his people could prosper...if she designed the right home for them.

All her efforts would go toward finding just the right balance between functional design and the natural world around them. She would put all her energy into making this the best set of structures she had ever dreamed into reality. They would stand the test of time and help Mark rebuild his culture, his Clan and their way of life. It was a noble cause, even if nobody on the outside would ever know what she had done here.

She would know. The jaguars would know. It was enough.

She could see it now in her mind's eye. As Mark continued

to speak of his dreams for the location, Shelly's imagination was sparking into a flame of images that she would put on paper to show him. She couldn't wait to get sketching. In fact...

Shelly opened the travel case she'd brought with her and started to let the images out onto the paper. These weren't the detailed drawings she would do later, but rough pencil sketches of what she saw while Mark spoke. It was almost as if she was drawing the images from his words. A collaboration between his dreams and her talent for architecture were coming together on the pad she held in one hand while the other wielded a pencil like a magic wand, flying over the page.

Something unexpected. The outside of the community center had the image of the jaguar climbing down one side. Roof to ground was the back of the jaguar's spine, his paws extending along the ground to shelter a playground for the smallest children.

"Sweet Mother of All." The whisper of Mark's voice came to her over one shoulder. He sounded astonished. "I love this idea." His arm draped over her shoulder to trace the spine of the jaguar on the paper with something close to awe. "You have captured us."

She wasn't sure how exactly to take that last sentence. Did he mean she'd captured the essence of their aesthetic style? If so, great. But he could also have meant that she'd captured his attention in a more intimate way. If so...also great, but kind of scary too.

It was certain Mark Pepard had captivated her in every way, even on such short acquaintance. He was, by far, the most magical man she knew. The most magical she would ever know, she was sure. He'd introduced her to concepts she hadn't even known were possible. Shapeshifters. Magic. Hidden lairs for an amazing people.

Her life had taken a huge turn the moment she'd decided to share a taxi with a stranger. If not for that tenuous connection with the man who had tried to assassinate Mark, she might never have gotten close enough to meet him. And if they'd never met…

She didn't like to think about that. He'd altered her perceptions of reality so greatly in just a couple of days. The world was so much bigger now. She hated to think about going back to a time when she wasn't aware of the magic all around her. It was as if she'd been incomplete until now. Mark, and the discovery of his dual nature and the existence of shifters, had changed her forever. Making her…more than she had ever been before.

And it truly felt like they were only just beginning. Her instinct said there was more coming. More magic. More revelations. More changes. Just…more. She didn't know whether to be eager or afraid, but some small voice inside her spoke reassurance to her soul. Like this was the way things were always supposed to have been. Like she should trust the universe to put her where she was supposed to be, when she was supposed to be there. Right here, right now.

The way they were standing, she was almost in his arms. In fact, if she leaned back just the tiniest bit, she would feel his warm chest against her back. It took a lot of willpower to resist the temptation.

"You think it's okay? Not too obvious?" she asked, hearing the breathless note in her own voice.

"It's perfect. They're going to love it." He moved away, taking his warmth with him. A little pang of regret went through her before she made herself focus on his words.

"They? Are you putting my work up for approval before a board or something?" The question came out somewhat inelegantly, but he didn't seem to mind.

"I may be the Alpha, but the whole Clan is going to have to live here. I've got a council of sorts that will have veto power over most things, but I doubt any of them could find any fault with your artistic ideas if that's the direction you're going in." He gestured to the sketch pad, still in her hands. "They're more interested in functionality and things a human architect—no offense intended—might not factor in for our beast halves." He looked a bit sheepish but never lost that air of command that came so naturally to him. It was incredibly sexy.

"That makes sense," she allowed. "I've certainly never designed anything with big cats in mind before, so I could definitely use some help there to make sure my ideas are workable."

At that moment, Mark's phone rang. He lifted the device from his belt and looked at the number, then looked at her. "I have to take this. Don't wander too far. I'll be right back."

He stepped away, already answering the phone as he walked away. She supposed it was either business or Clan related, and she tried not to take offense that he obviously didn't want her to hear his side of the conversation. He turned to look at her when he was far enough away that she couldn't hear anything. His eyes followed her as she moved around the site, taking measurements and making notes.

She had enough to begin with—at least for the community center. He'd given her a detailed description and walked out the boundaries of where he wanted it to be. He was thinking on a grand scale, which made her job much more interesting. She didn't often get to design large multi-use structures like this. It would be a challenge and a lot of fun at the same time.

Shelly sat on a stack of lumber that had a camouflage tarp over the top of it and set to work. She let her pencil fly once more, referencing the landscape and drawing out the view from the ground at this angle with the building she envisioned center stage. She repeated the process from another vantage point across the way.

Whoever Mark was talking to, the conversation was in-depth. Or perhaps, he had made multiple calls in the time it took her to sketch out her ideas. She wasn't really sure. She sort of lost track of time when she was in the zone, like this.

She was just finishing up her last drawing, sitting on yet another tarp-covered stack of building supplies, when she became aware of the sound of tiny paws on plastic. If she wasn't much mistaken, Kensi, or another child about the same size as the little jaguar cub she had met this morning, was trying—not too successfully—to sneak up on Shelly.

She turned her head and came face to face with a curious-eyed jaguar cub. He was a little bigger than Kensi, but still a baby compared to the full-grown jaguars she had seen here and there roaming in the woods around the site.

"Well, hello there," she said to the child, who jumped back a few steps on being discovered. She tried to inject friendliness into her tone, not wanting to scare the child further. "Did you want to see what I'm drawing?" Slowly, Shelly raised the sketch pad to the youngster's eye level, and sure enough, the fascinating amber eyes moved to focus on yet another angle of the community center she was planning.

"Miguel!" a man's voice came from a few yards away, and the cub looked up with a guilty expression on his furry little face. The man saw him and moved closer, smiling at Shelly. "I'm sorry if he's bothering you."

"Oh, he's no bother at all," Shelly reassured the man. "I'm Shelly, the architect. I'm just sketching a few designs for the new Clan hall."

"I'm Julio, lead carpenter on this job, and you've met my son, Miguel. My mate, Leena, is on the other side of the site, looking for him, but I expect she'll be along soon." He didn't offer to shake hands, but she didn't take offense. Maybe that was some kind of shifter thing. She was in their world now. She'd have to learn their customs.

"Well, if you're lead on this job, and the council approves my designs, I suppose we'll be working together for a bit," she said, though she really wasn't sure how involved Mark wanted her to be past the design stage. That was something they had yet to discuss.

Julio didn't say anything to that. He just nodded. Hmm. Perhaps he was reserving judgment about her. It wouldn't be the first time she'd had to prove herself, and her designs, to skeptical tradesmen. She offered him the sketch pad.

"These are just a few rough drawings, but this is the direction I'm thinking of going in for the community center," she told him.

He took the sketch pad with raised eyebrows and a delicate touch that made her think—nonsensically—that he probably thought the pad would bite him if he grabbed it too hard. She had to stop herself from grinning at her own thoughts.

As Julio paged through her sketches, his expression changed dramatically. He went from skeptical to impressed, if she was reading him right. She felt like crowing as he handed the pad back to her.

"These are really good. The Clan is going to love this," Julio told her.

Was he getting choked up? This big brute of a man certainly sounded as if he had a big frog in his throat.

"Thank you," she replied quietly, giving the man a moment to collect himself. "I tried to capture the spirit of this place, and of your people. I hope to do them both justice in a design that will last many lifetimes."

That, right there, was why she loved architecture. It was her chance to leave something tangible, and hopefully beautiful, in this world for generations to come. Like none of her other projects, this one would do that in a big way. If she got it right. There was a lot riding on her imagination and ability to come up with something both practical and beautiful.

"I think you have the start of something amazing," Julio went on to say. "The Goddess truly blessed us when She put you in our Alpha's path." He paused as she looked at him with surprise.

They believed in the Goddess? Not the Catholic faith that dominated much of South America?

Hmm. That was interesting. Shelly's father had always insisted that the Howells hailed from a sect of Goddess worshipers, and if that faith had seen their ancestors rise to power, then it was better to stick with the old ways.

As a result, Shelly had been raised in the old ways. They celebrated what most people called *pagan* holidays, which usually coincided with the more traditional religious festivities that most people in the United States celebrated. They did so quietly, of course. Their faith was their own business, her father had said many times. Nobody else's.

Shelly hadn't minded. For some reason, she'd always felt closer to the female deity her father had taught her about than the male deity her friends had talked about on occasion. The Goddess seemed present to her in a way she couldn't properly explain, but that instinct of hers, once again, told her it was the right way for her.

Shelly found Julio's reaction to her design interesting. He seemed truly touched by what she had been envisioning, which gratified her to no end.

"What is that area there, by the jaguar's paw?" Julio asked, peering down at the sketch pad in her hands where she'd been roughing in areas that would be fully detailed later.

"I thought the forearms and paws could act as low safety walls around a play area for the smaller children," she told him. "I'm just not sure what kinds of gym equipment might be appropriate for your children. I assume things they can climb on, though not too high, of course. Maybe swings and perhaps a sprinkler area considering how hot it must get here at times."

"That sounds about right, but my sister Helena would know more about exactly what you'll need for each age level. She's a teacher. Or you can ask my Leena about what our cub likes. Ah." He turned, revealing the fact that Mark was walking back to Shelly, a tall brunette woman at his side. "Here she comes now, with my cousin. *Mi amor*, come see what this talented lady has come up with for our *niños*." He directed the last part to his wife.

Introductions were made as Julio leaned over to pick up Miguel, still in kitten form, to hold in his arms. Shelly liked the woman right, off and Leena was very enthusiastic about the planned playground. They started talking particulars about what kinds of equipment and toys each age group might need. Low balance beams for the youngest were sufficient and safe for their four-legged forms. Wider tree trunks a little higher up were good for the toddlers, though nothing taller than five feet or so, for safety.

Older kids climbed higher, and for them, Mark was pushing for an actual climbing wall, though there would have to be two separate courses—one designed for humans, which could be vertical with the standard holds that were employed by many commercial climbing facilities, along with the usual harnesses and safety gear—and one built with big cats in mind. It would have to be more of a natural slope, which Shelly thought could be built right into the side of the building itself.

The afternoon passed in a flurry of ideas and sketches as Shelly firmed up her initial design for the community center. Eventually, Miguel, Julio and Leena said their farewells, promising to see Shelly again at dinner back at the mansion. At which point, Mark took her by the hand and led her to a somewhat secluded area near one of the sheltering walls of rock that had once been the fiery heart of a living volcano.

"What is this?" she asked, the slight tremor in her voice betraying her feelings.

For some reason, this place resonated with her in a special way. The entire site felt like coming home, in an odd way, but this particular place had a magic about it all its own.

"This is the spot where I will build my home," he told her. "I want you to design this, as well. A place for me and my family. A place where the Alpha can be just another man. Just another jaguar. And his mate can be happy." He turned to her, and he was a lot closer than she realized.

She reached out to steady herself on the uneven ground, and he put his hands out to catch her. A sudden wave of dizziness had hit her when he looked at her with blazing gold swirling in his eyes. It was the gold of his jaguar. The wildness of his spirit showing through.

She tried to understand his words, but the feel of his warm fingers on her arms and the closeness of his body made thinking difficult. Feeling was easier at the moment, and her desire was peaking in a way that was both unprecedented and a bit frightening. But fear would not hold her back. Not this time. Not with this man. She knew, somehow, that he would not betray her, or belittle her, or make light of her feelings.

No, this was a serious man with grown-up sensibilities. No matter what the tabloids said about him, everything she'd seen to this point indicated a steady, responsible, caring man who did have a playful side but was also loyal to those around him and loving toward those he called his family.

She admired him in a way she had never admired any other man. And she was drawn to him. There was no doubt about his allure. The chemistry between them felt like it would be explosive when they finally combined.

"I want you to design a home here that you could be happy in, *querida*," he whispered to her, drawing her ever closer. His eyes bore into hers as his lips descended, and then, he was kissing her in a way that felt very much as if he was staking some sort of claim.

She was all for it. Whatever he wanted. As long as he kept kissing her like this. That was the last coherent thought she had before the ability to think at all disappeared completely.

He took her down to the ground, and she was glad to go with him, loving the way he mastered her and seemed to watch for her slightest response. He was learning what she liked in a methodical way that spoke of experience, but also of care.

Her shirt was pushed up and then it was just gone, and she felt the warm kiss of moist tropical air on her skin, followed by the wetness of Mark's mouth as he blazed a trail of sucking kisses over her neck and chest. When he teased her nipples with his teeth, she had to bite back a whimper of delight. He certainly did know how to please.

Then, somehow, her pants were gone, as well. She had a lucid thought about the time he slid between her naked thighs, but it was gone in the next moment as his tongue pierced her center in a warm invasion that made her squeal. She might've given a thought to all the men and cats she'd seen crawling all over the large building site—if she'd had a coherent thought to give. As it was, she was focused solely on what Mark was doing to her. A little more of that…right…there… And she came like a rocket, a guttural groan of release torn from her throat.

He rose up, claiming her lips with his once more as he then slid into her slick warmth, possessing her utterly. She hadn't meant to have sex with him just yet, but as she felt him begin to move inside her, she couldn't really understand why she had wanted to deny herself this amazing pleasure. Mark was magic. His movements were knowing and perfect. His timing impeccable.

And if he got a little out of control there toward the end, she was even more turned on by the fact that she could make him lose it like that. Talk about sexy. *Rawr*.

Shelly clung to him as he rocked them to the stars and back. Her fingers explored the muscles of his shoulders and chest, loving the feel of him. He was so big and warm, and hard-bodied in a way she hadn't really expected a multi-billionaire to be. Then again, he was a shifter. She'd seen his cat. She knew the jaguar was a sleek, muscled creature of instinct and cunning. Just like his human side.

She marveled at his gentleness. That was unexpected. He rolled them so that he lay on the ground, and she covered him like a living blanket.

"I'm sorry if I rushed you, *mi amor*, but I couldn't wait." He was still inside her. Less rigid now, after his climax, but still a presence that made her take notice.

She placed nibbling kisses on his collarbone, her head resting on his shoulder. She was perfectly comfortable on top of him, though the thought crossed her mind that maybe she was too heavy for him. She would have moved…if she'd had the energy. But he didn't seem to mind. She figured a man as sure of himself as Mark would put her where he wanted her, and it sure felt like he wanted her on top of him right now. Thank goodness.

"I don't mind," she told him sleepily. "I liked it."

He chuckled, a low throaty sound that vibrated through his chest. "Just *like*?" His hand ran down her spine, raising goose bumps of renewed desire in their path. "I'm going to have to try harder then."

"If you try any harder, I might just faint from the pleasure," she told him honestly, starting to feel frisky again as his hands continued to run over her body, pausing here and there to tease and tantalize.

She felt his cock stir within her. Impossible, right? It was too soon. But he wasn't entirely human… Maybe that meant… Oh, yes…it certainly did.

This time, she took the lead. She sat up, impaling herself more fully as his cock hardened to a steel rod within her. Oh, yeah. He felt so good.

She began to move on him, her hands on his shoulders for support, her knees on the ground on either side of his narrow hips. She had never been so brazen before. Making love in broad daylight, knowing there were other people in the area who might happen upon them at any time.

Hell, they were shifters. They probably could hear what was going on, or smell it or something. They had super-senses. But somehow, that didn't bother her. Miguel and his family had left the site. There were no other children around. Just a bunch of big, burly members of the construction crews and the men who had chosen to prowl around in their big cat forms.

Would she mind if they saw her fucking their boss into the next galaxy?

What kind of thought was that? Shelly had never been into exhibitionism. But there was something tantalizing in that forbidden thought…

Mark's hands rose to cup her breasts, playing with her nipples, pinching with just the right pressure. Her head fell back as a moan tore through her body. Shit. No way those sensitive shifters hadn't heard that mating call. Was she *trying* to draw attention?

The honest truth was that maybe she was. Some instinct

inside her wanted the jaguars to witness her claiming of their Alpha, though why her mind phrased it exactly that way, she had no idea. But…her instincts had never steered her wrong so far.

Fire arced through her body as a small climax hit her. She saw sparkles of fiery light before her eyes, but wasn't sure if they were real or some kind of optical illusion. Probably the latter. Mark was the magic man. He had proved himself capable of making her feel all sorts of new sensations that she'd never experienced before.

She looked up and met the blue eyes of Heinrich, the pilot. He was standing a few yards away. Watching.

A secret thrill shot through her body as she turned her head slightly.

And met the steely gaze of Nick, the bodyguard who had been so mean to her on first acquaintance. He was staring at her now, his eyes filled with the gold of his cat.

More intense vibrations went through her, driving her pleasure higher. Holy shit. She *was* an exhibitionist!

She turned her head again and found more men watching. Some were naked, as if they'd just shifted from cat to human. And some of those had their hands on their cocks. Hard cocks. Excited by the view.

And that excited her more.

Mark pinched her nipple, drawing her attention back to him.

"Don't let them trouble you. They are here to bear witness. That's all," he told her. She didn't really understand what he meant but was beyond caring as his other hand went to her clit.

A few delicate strokes and she went higher than she had before, crying out his name as she came and came. She felt his warmth erupting into her, like the volcano in which they lay must have done millennia ago on a much grander scale.

The heat rose in her, scalding her in the most intense pleasure of her life. Sparks flew between them, shooting from her fingers into the volcanic rock beneath the forest floor.

Absorbed into it. Welcomed home.

Or maybe it was all an illusion. Shelly couldn't be sure what was real and what was fantasy anymore. Mark had made the impossible come to life, and the pleasure he gave her as they came together fuzzed the edges of reality too much for her to comprehend exactly what was happening.

She collapsed on top of him, aware of the jaguar eyes on them. She knew they'd been seen, and that knowledge made her feel like a cat herself. A very satisfied cat who had just claimed the cream.

CHAPTER 9

Shelly didn't know how she got back to the Jeep. Mark must have carried her, though she had no recollection of it. That last orgasm had knocked her out. Literally.

Something earth shattering had happened there, but she wasn't exactly sure what it was all about. She'd have to think about it later—when her brain had begun to function normally again. For now, she was toast. Happy toast. Satisfied toast. But still toast.

What had just happened had blown her mind, but she was okay with it. Surprisingly, Mark brought out the wild child in her that she'd never known existed. She kind of liked the woman she was when she was with him.

Uninhibited. Wild. Free.

None of those words had ever applied to her before. No, Shelly had always played by the rules. She'd been a good girl from a good family. Respectable. Proper. Almost uptight.

The old Shelly would never have made love in the grass with a circle of strange men looking on. The new Shelly reveled in her new freedom. Not that she wanted such displays to become commonplace, but she had sensed something special about what had just happened. Something life changing. Destiny altering.

Or maybe she was just caught up in the fantasy. Magical

Mark had shown her things she'd never experienced before. He'd given her a gift. One that she would never, in this lifetime, forget.

Whether there was to be a repeat performance or not remained to be seen. She certainly hoped there would be. If she had anything to say about it, she'd lock him in her bedroom and throw away the key. His kisses had been addictive enough, but his lovemaking was something else altogether.

He drove them back down the mountain while Shelly dozed in the passenger seat. Mark had helped her dress. She remembered that. And he'd buckled her into the Jeep, adjusting her seat so that she could recline a bit more. He'd also stowed her pad and the small portfolio she kept it in behind her seat. She'd been awake enough to remember that much, but the rest of the trip was accomplished in a bit of a daze.

She knew in her heart that her response wasn't quite normal, but it also wasn't dangerous. It was just…new.

"Hold on, *querida*, we'll have you at the mansion in no time. And then, I want *Abuela* to look at you." She could hear worry in his tone, but she didn't have the energy to wonder too much about it.

"I'm okay," she tried to tell him, but her words were slurred. It sounded like she was drunk or something. Odd.

He made calming sounds as he maneuvered the Jeep down the mountain trail. It seemed like no time at all before they pulled up in front of the mansion, and she was in his arms once more. Mark carried her up the steps as if she weighed nothing at all, and then into the room that she'd been shown earlier. He laid her on the bed, and it wasn't a minute before an old woman came into the room.

Shelly was confused, but still groggy, so she didn't question it too much. Mark welcomed the old woman and led her to Shelly's side.

Shelly didn't really register what happened next until a jolt of…electricity? Lightning? Some sort of magic?

It lit her up from inside, shocking her system into rhythm once more. Like a light switch had been thrown, she started to become more aware of her surroundings and the strange old woman seated at her bedside.

Mark hovered over the old lady's shoulder, his expression concerned. His gaze sought Shelly's, and she could see the relief in his eyes as her vision cleared. Things began to come back into focus, and the hazy feeling departed.

"Was it your first time loosing your magic?" the old lady asked her. The question made no sense.

"My magic?" The old woman's words didn't make sense...and yet... "I don't have magic. Do I?"

Abuela laughed. "*Chica*, it is flame I sense in your heart. Fire is your element and sparks your nature. You are well suited to this island and to the jaguar. Perhaps that is what woke your sleeping talent."

"Fire?" It all made a strange sort of sense. "I felt sparks..."

"I felt them too. They scorched, but did not burn. And you released them into the ground. The obsidian heated beneath us and welcomed the fire magic like an old friend." Mark was rather poetic when he wanted to be, she thought.

"The magic went to reinforce the wards I've already put in place. You added a great deal to the protections on our new home, *mis hijos*," *Abuela* told them. "I will pray to the Mother of All in thanks for your strength. It will do our Clan good."

"The Mother of All," Shelly repeated, smiling. "I like that. Is that what shifters call Her? The Goddess?"

"You believe in the Goddess?" Mark asked in a shocked tone.

Shelly smiled. "I was raised with the Goddess. My father said the Howells have worshiped Her since the family began, and he wasn't about to change things now. But I've never heard Her called that before. The Mother of All," she repeated. "It's a beautiful description."

Abuela nodded in agreement. "Do you also have this saying—that the Goddess works in mysterious ways?"

"I may have heard something like that a time or two," Shelly agreed, chuckling faintly.

The old woman laughed as she stood from the chair. "I think I see Her hand in this union, since our Clan is sworn to the Goddess and Her Light. Now, I shocked you into wakefulness," she said carefully. "I think you were drunk on your new power and drained yourself a bit too low when you released it into the earth. You must learn what power level is best for your health. I can help you, if you wish, when you are recovered. You will sleep deep tonight, but you should be fine in the morning. Call me if you have any problems, Alpha. I will have Marie send up a tray for your dinner and make your apologies to the others." *Abuela* winked at Shelly with a smile. "They'll understand. It's not every day a new power awakens or a mate bond is forged. There will be dancing in the jungle tonight."

With that rather odd declaration, the old lady left. Mark saw her to the door then returned and sat on the side of the bed, taking one of Shelly's hands in his. He kissed the back and held it to his chest. She could feel his heart beating against her palm and knew the moment was a significant one, though she didn't fully understand what was going on. She was still a little foggy on the details.

"Don't ever scare me like that again, *querida*," he admonished in a gentle voice.

"I didn't mean to scare you," she protested weakly. "I still don't really know what happened."

"You rocked my world. That's what happened," he told her, grinning widely. "And then, you all but passed out after the most amazing light show I've ever witnessed. There were sparks shooting from your fingertips."

"Really?" She held up her free hand and examined it. Looked okay to her.

"Really." He lifted the hand he still held and kissed each fingertip in a gesture she found highly romantic. "It tickled when the sparks hit my skin. It made the climax so much...more... Just more intense than anything I've ever experienced. I knew being with my mate would be special, but this was…" He shook his head. "I don't have adequate words to describe it."

"That good, eh?" A little thrill of feminine pride stirred in her middle, though she'd never felt anything of the kind before. Mark was helping her experience all sorts of new and exciting things.

"Seriously, though…" He placed her hand back over his heart, his fingers linked loosely with hers. "We should probably figure out where your wild magic comes from. There must've been a mage or some kind of magical being somewhere back in your family line."

"I doubt my father would know anything, but there might be some old records of ancestors back at his house," she offered. She really couldn't see that her somewhat aloof father would have any idea about magic, but then, stranger things had happened. Just this afternoon, in fact.

A gentle knock on the door preceded its opening. Janice entered, carrying a large tray laden with delicious-smelling dishes. Only then did Shelly realize she was really hungry. She sat up in bed with Mark's help as Janice set everything up on a folding table that had wheels on the bottom that she retrieved from the closet.

Janice left with a shy smile, and Mark served them both. They shared an intimate meal and didn't speak of anything too weighty until they had finished their main courses and were looking at the selection of sweets Janice had brought.

"You know…" Mark began, his low tone alerting her to the fact that he was changing the mood of their conversation. "Something very special happened today. I know you're human, and I've been trying not to rush you, but you're my mate, *querida*. That means something very special to my kind. Today only solidified the fact that we were meant to be."

"You believe in fated mates? That there's just one person meant specifically for you?" she asked, curious.

He nodded slowly. "We do. And we spend most of our lives searching for that perfect mate. Sadly, it doesn't happen for everyone, but for those who are blessed—as I have been blessed to find you—the promise of a lifetime of happiness with a perfect match is assured. I am only concerned that you may not feel the same since you are human. Although… You probably aren't completely human if that light show is anything to go by." He tilted his head and gave her a gentle smile. "You have magic of your own."

"I'm not sure I agree with that. I've never been…magical." Even as she said the words, she thought about the hunches, and what she called instinct, that she had learned to rely on throughout her life. As far as she knew, normal people didn't have that sixth sense that had steered her in the right direction time after time.

"I saw it with my own eyes. And felt it. You have power, *mi amor*. Perhaps it was latent up to this point, but you won't be able to stuff that genie back in its bottle. You'll have to train to control it and temper it to your will."

"I'm not sure about any of this, but if you're right about me having some kind of fire magic, then I can definitely see your point about controlling it." She yawned, the stresses of the day catching up with her.

"You are tired," Mark observed. "We can discuss this tomorrow. For now…" He took the plates away and piled everything on the tray then rolled the table to an out-of-the-way spot near the door. He then turned back to the bed and started unbuttoning his shirt. "We will sleep. And I will hold you through the night and make sure you are all right."

Her body perked up a bit at the sight of his bare chest, but she really was exhausted. Her spirit might be willing, but her flesh was weak at this point. It craved sleep more than Mark's irresistible body…for the moment.

Still, she couldn't help salivating just a little as he stripped. Just for her.

And then, he climbed into bed with her, spooning her from behind and tugging the covers up to cover them both.

Sometime in the night, he must have removed her clothing, too, because she woke naked in his arms, in the hour just before dawn. They came together, a slow, soundless loving. A meeting of bodies and hearts in the quiet of the darkness that still shrouded the world. Then, she dozed again.

The next time she woke, the sun was shining, and Mark was gone from the bed. She could still feel his presence, though, and she knew he hadn't gone far, or for long.

She showered and dressed, heading out into the house in search of Mark. Or breakfast. Preferably both.

She ran into Leena and Miguel, who was in his human form this time, in the hallway, and they exchanged greetings. It was Leena who told Shelly where to find Mark. Apparently, he and Julio, Leena's mate, were having a big discussion about the building project, and Shelly would be most welcome to join them, according to Leena.

Following the other woman's directions to something called the Morning Room, Shelly knocked somewhat hesitantly before entering. She wasn't exactly sure she would be as welcome as Leena thought, but when she poked her head in the door, Mark was all smiles as he stood from the table. He ushered her inside and even pulled out a chair for her next to his.

He'd greeted her with a kiss, right in front of the other men in the room, and she realized they probably all had heard the tale of their sexcapade the day before—if they hadn't been there in person. Shelly felt the blush flood her cheeks with warmth but kept her head as high as she could. She had nothing to be ashamed of. She was a consenting adult, and everything she'd done with Mark in the jungle had felt absolutely right at the time.

She might be a little embarrassed now, but there was no use crying over spilt milk. And besides, shifters probably had different rules than other people, right? She certainly hoped so. Otherwise, this job might get a little uncomfortable.

"*Mi amor*, you met Julio yesterday. And this is Keith. He built the warehouse using Redstone plans," Mark said, then proceeded to go around the table, introducing the half dozen men who each had some part to play in the planned and ongoing construction on the island.

What followed was a lively discussion of what had been done so far and where they planned to go from here. Shelly noticed Mark had taken her sketch book from her room and showed a couple of the designs she'd been playing with the day before to the others. She didn't mind, though normally she would have preferred to only show finished drawings to her clients. But, of course, nothing about this job was normal.

When she'd entered the room, she'd been afraid things might feel awkward after what they probably had witnessed the day before, but it wasn't. Much to her relief, they didn't make her feel strange. In fact, they treated her like an old friend—a somewhat different attitude than she had received on arrival. It was almost as if she had passed some sort of test and was now somehow a bit more accepted among these secretive people.

Janice came in with trays of food, placing them in the middle of the table, but everyone waited for Shelly to select her breakfast first. It was strange, that, but very considerate. She was hungry enough to fill a plate for herself, but there was plenty left, and as soon as she had hers, the men descended on the platters like locusts.

They spent the next hour eating, talking and going over her designs. They also talked about the improvements that could be made to the warehouse she had mentioned the day before. Shelly was really pleased with how cooperative and knowledgeable these men were proving to be. Working with them would be a pleasure, if this meeting was anything to go by.

"Do you have any women on your construction crews?" Shelly didn't feel too intimidated being the only woman in the room, but at one point, she felt it only fair to raise the question.

Mark laughed. "Actually, we have quite a few," he replied as all the other men smiled. "In fact, while Julio might be lead carpenter on the Clan hall project, it's Leena who is the project manager. She's the one who will be doing all the oversight, scheduling, and generally keeping everybody on their toes."

"My mate is hell on wheels in a pretty pink plastic safety helmet," Julio agreed with a wide grin. "She has more experience than I do when it comes to construction. She is a civil engineer by training and worked for a few of the biggest human construction companies as a project manager, among other titles, before we got together."

"She was a perfect fit for the project here, and I asked her to give up her career on the mainland to work for the Clan," Mark put in. "Julio is representing her at this meeting, since it's just a preliminary discussion and she had a prior commitment with their son's teacher."

Julio shrugged. "The move here worked out well for all of us. We both wanted to be close for our cub, and he can grow up here out in the open, not needing to hide his dual nature. It's a blessing, truly. Miguel is thriving, as are the other children already on the island."

"That's why getting construction underway quickly is so important," Mark agreed. "We want to bring as many families here as want to come. We want this to be a place where the next generation can grow up in peace, out in the open, able to explore in either of their forms without fear of discovery."

Shelly began to understand how very dedicated all of these people—not just Mark—were to this project. They shared his vision and strong desire to make it a reality.

When the meeting broke up, it was just before noon. Mark suggested a stroll on the veranda, and Shelly was glad to get outside, even if it was hot out there. The island had some very refreshing breezes, and in the short time she had been there, it had impressed her as a tropical paradise.

Mark took her hand as they walked slowly to the balustrade. The view from up here showed them the small harbor and that very reflective warehouse they had discussed at length during the meeting. If Shelly had her way, the thing would be coated with a more inviting skin ASAP. One that wouldn't act like a mirror sending the blinding rays of the sun toward the mansion at least once a day.

"*Mi amor*, I have a favor to ask," Mark said, sounding almost hesitant. She stopped and looked up at him.

"What is it?" She was concerned by his reluctance.

"Would you be upset with me if I asked you to stay another night on the island? I know I promised that you'd be home later today, but something has come up, and I really need to stay. I ask that you stay with me, since my heart will not rest easy if you are on the mainland and I am here."

Was that all? Sure, she hadn't planned on a second night on the island, but it really wasn't that big a deal.

"All right," she agreed quietly. "To be honest, I'm still feeling a little woozy from yesterday, so I don't mind staying put for another day."

His smile was both relieved and concerned. "If you have any discomfort from the magic, *Abuela* can help. You shouldn't hesitate to consult her. Or Judy and Jim, who are both healers. They can help with more mundane complaints. And if there's anything I can do, all you have to do is say the word."

"No, I'm fine. Really. Just tired from whatever that was yesterday." She still couldn't bring herself to believe it was actual magic. She was human. Not magical at all. Right?

"Good. Because we're about to be welcoming some very important company. Their visit is why I have to stay. We're opening formal relations between my Clan and the tigers. That's what the phone call was about yesterday. The tiger Clan has had a rough time of it lately too, and they have a new king and queen. Allowing them to visit here is a first step toward an alliance that could help us both rebuild our Clans."

"Seriously? Shifter royalty?" She was a little mystified by the idea but also very intrigued.

"Yeah, the other big cat Clans organize themselves a little differently than us jaguars. Many of them migrated away from their countries of origin toward Western Europe around the time of the Renaissance. We've always been folks who try to be where the action is, and back in those times, it was centered in Italy and France for our kind."

Shelly was impressed. "You mentioned some of this before," she remembered. "The tigers and lions have a king and queen, not an Alpha like your Clan."

"Oh, the monarchs are very, very Alpha, I'm sure, but they also formalized their positions into monarchies with all the trappings that were so popular back then in that part of the world. We're a bit less formal. More tribal, still, I guess." He shrugged elegantly. "The Mother of All also plays a part. It is said the Tig'Ra and Tig'Ren, the tiger king and queen, are Goddess-touched. They, alone, among tiger shifters have white fur."

"White tigers," Shelly breathed. She knew, even among regular tigers, the white ones were incredibly rare.

Mark nodded. "Though the story circulating about the new tiger king says he was born *tigre d'or*—a golden tiger— and was changed by the hand of the Goddess so he could reclaim the throne from a total bastard named Gisli, who just about ran that Clan into the ground. Gisli was a terrible businessman, and an even worse king. He abused his people, and frankly, I don't think his claim to the throne was true. I met him just once, and he made my skin crawl. I refused to have anything to do with him after that single encounter."

"But this new guy sounds better?" Shelly asked, surprisingly interested in shifter politics.

"I've had him checked out from afar. Everything about him reads as on the level. He was a Royal Guard before he mated with the tiger princess-in-exile."

"Wait. The monarchs were in exile?" Shelly was trying hard to follow the story.

"Gisli was the younger brother of the old king. Somehow, he forced the rightful king and queen into fleeing with their only daughter. Their son and heir had already been murdered, so I kind of understand why they would give up and go into hiding to protect their remaining child." Mark's expression held compassion. "Regardless, Gisli set himself up as steward to the Clan in the king's absence. Eventually, he pretty much took over and made himself a monarch anyway. But then, last year, there was a challenge fight, and the former Royal Guard proved himself worthy and took the title of Tig'Ra, the princess, his mate, at his side."

"If he was a Royal Guard, was he guarding the king's family in exile?" Shelly wanted to know.

"No, actually, it's rumored that he got his training among the *pantera noir*—literally, black panthers. They're mostly black leopards, but I look a bit like one of those guys when I shift, so I've been mistaken for one of them on occasion. I use that to my advantage because they're like the ninjas of the shifter world. Highly secretive. Always hidden. And highly skilled. If the tiger king was accepted by them as a youngster, and trained in their ways, he has to be a formidable fighter, and an expert at stealth. They say he was Royal Guard to the *Nyx*, the *pantera noir* queen. I hear she's also newly mated—to a human."

"So, if you make friends with the tiger king, you might possibly also open up a channel to these black panthers," Shelly guessed, seeing the advantages.

Mark smiled at her deduction. "Exactly. You see why it's important I'm here to greet the royal couple personally. They won't stay long, and they may not get past the mansion—depending on how the initial meeting goes—but this is a critical meeting for myself, and for the Clan as a whole. Plus, there are things I can do to help them. Gisli ran the tiger Clan's businesses into the ground, like I said. I can help them rebuild. Some of my companies are positioned in the same markets, and we could do some beneficial deals to help them get back on their feet financially."

"Win-win," Shelly grinned. "I like that."

"Let's hope it works out. I'd appreciate it if you would help me entertain them. The new queen lived among humans most of her life, they say. I think she'd enjoy your company. It also might help make me seem a bit less…threatening, shall we say…if I have a beautiful woman on my arm, whom I am desperately trying to convince to be my mate."

He turned her then, taking her in his arms. She saw his kiss coming and didn't move away. She would take all he would give her physically while they were together. She just wasn't so sure she could be what he needed long-term. How could a regular human being be his mate? How could she help him run a Clan of shapeshifters when she wasn't one? Would his people even accept her long-term? She was very much afraid they would not.

"Is that what you're doing? Trying to convince me?" She smiled, but her thoughts were confused. "Are you sure you really want that?"

CHAPTER 10

Mark leaned down and kissed her, just once. Moving only far enough away to look into her eyes, he spoke in an intimate tone.

"I've never been surer of anything else in my life. I want you for my mate, Shelly. I know you're human—and magical, though you still seem to be in denial about that—but I hope you can feel the same need. The same draw. The same imperative that we must be together." He held both of her hands in his, against his beating heart. "If you agree to be my mate, I will love you, and only you, for the rest of our lives. I will never stray, and I will be the best mate I can possibly be. I promise."

Whoa. Her head was spinning again, and it wasn't just from that light show she'd been part of yesterday. Mark was getting a little too intense for her. She was so confused about everything. She needed a little room to think.

She was saved from having to make a reply by the arrival of the security guy named Mario. He had a pained look on his face while he apologized for interrupting, but he brought news. The tigers had arrived.

Mark was suddenly all business. She realized how important this visit was to him by the way he reacted, and she vowed, then and there, to help him win over these shifter monarchs in any way that she could. Mark was a good guy, and his people deserved all the help they could get. Whatever little thing Shelly could do to help that, she would do.

"Is everything ready?" Mark asked Mario as they all headed back into the mansion.

"As ready as we can be," came the quick reply. "Janice is setting up refreshments in the back parlor and said to tell you that, if they want to stay overnight, the best guest suite is ready and waiting."

"Let's see how this goes first," Mark replied as they walked into the house. "I don't want to jinx anything by thinking too far ahead. They may have a schedule to keep, which wouldn't surprise me. Plus, it's a first visit to unknown territory. They'll be cautious." Mark ran a hand down his shirt, as if searching for wrinkles, then he turned to Shelly. "Do I look okay?"

She thought he looked perfect. Of course, she always thought that. Mark was one of those lucky individuals who looked good in anything and always seemed to have stepped off the pages of a magazine. He was just that good looking. Male model handsome with an intellect matched by few. He was the whole package.

But she took his question seriously. "How formal is this?" she asked, wondering if his neat polo shirt and khakis were appropriate.

"Business casual, I'd guess," he stated. "Any intel on what they're wearing?" he asked Mario, quickly turning back to the other man.

"Golf shirt and jeans for the male. Jeans and a T-shirt for the female. A little less than business casual, but still neat, is what Lucinda reports," Mario said, tapping a small earpiece Shelly just noticed as he drew attention to it. "They're coming up the walk from the landing strip now. ETA five minutes. And you should know, Kensi is missing again. I think she got curious and went down the path to see what all the fuss was about. She's been doing that more and more, according to Judy. She's going down to try to find her now."

"I don't think the tiger king or his lady would harm her," Mark said, then looked to Shelly as if for confirmation.

"They're civilized people, aren't they? And if they hurt a baby, these aren't people you'll want to deal with at all," Shelly said immediately.

"We'd better get out there. Maybe we can avoid an incident." Mark looked worried, and Shelly caught the tension in the air. She raced out of the house with him, Mario on their heels.

They took off down the path, slowing only at the bends in the path to peer out cautiously before they hit another straightaway. They didn't want to look like they were rushing to intercede before Kensi possibly intercepted the newcomers, but they also wanted to get to her first, if at all possible.

They had just slowed for another curve when the approaching party came into view. A beautiful woman with big blue eyes and luxurious blonde hair was holding a familiar jaguar cub. Kensi had indeed found the royal couple first, but from the way the woman was smiling as she cradled the baby jaguar, they had been worried for nothing.

It was clear Kensi had captured another heart. It was also clear that the tiger couple was not going to eat the child. Far from it. They both seemed indulgent toward her. Both were smiling as she batted at the king's tickling fingers. Shelly thought the image boded well for what was to come.

Mark breathed a sigh of relief and gathered himself before stepping forward to meet the tiger monarchs. His smile was broad and welcoming and perhaps a bit on the relieved side, but hopefully, the newcomers wouldn't notice that.

"I see you found our little escape artist," Mark said in a friendly tone as the two parties approached each other.

"She's adorable," the woman who must be the tiger queen said. "Is she yours?"

"She is mine the way all of my Clan are, but her parents should be along any moment, now that word is spreading that she's been found." Mark gestured toward the headset Lucinda sported. Apparently, the appearance of little Kensi on the walk up from the landing strip had already been reported, but Mark and Shelly were too far ahead of Mario to have heard the news.

"Aw, did you worry Mommy and Daddy?" the tiger queen spoke in a soft voice to the baby jaguar still held in her arms. "You shouldn't do that, sweetheart. You should always tell your parents where you're going so they can watch over you, okay?" She waited until the little jaguar head nodded up and down before snuggling the child close once more, calling her a *good girl*.

Right then, Shelly decided this woman was all right.

To say Mark was thrilled with the meeting wouldn't be overstating his reaction to the tiger monarchs. They were very nice people, in addition to being good rulers over their Clan. Mark had a chance to discuss Clan affairs in more detail than he'd expected with the tiger king, who'd asked Mark to call him Mitch.

Likewise, the queen was also on a first name basis with Shelly and Mark within the first five minutes of meeting. Mark knew she was a medical doctor in the human world and was known as Queen Gleda among the tiger Clan, but she'd asked them to call her by her nickname, Gina. Mark liked them both, and the feeling appeared to be mutual—at least as far as he could tell on first meeting. He thought, though, the relationship had begun on firm footing and would grow from there.

One thing that had surprised him was Mitch's knowledge about the geological foundations of the island. He'd come right out and asked if the volcano was still active. Funny thing was, he had directed his question to Shelly, which had struck Mark as odd.

"I only just came here yesterday for the first time," Shelly had replied. "I don't know all that much about the island yet."

"As far as we know, the volcano has been dormant for

centuries. Our shamans say we should not have any trouble for many years to come, which is why I chose this place," Mark added.

The Tig'Ra looked at him strangely for a moment, then seemed to make up his mind about something before he spoke again. "I suppose you know our place of power is in Iceland, right?" Mark nodded in answer as Mitch went on, "Thing is, our palace is built on the side of an active—a *very* active—volcano. I'm actually connected to it in some magical way that I don't completely understand. That's how I recognized the echoes of that power here. You might be able to tap into that, somehow, to help protect your people."

Mark was nonplussed. He'd never heard that about the tiger king, and he'd thought he had excellent intel on the tiger Clan in general. Apparently, there were still some secrets they'd managed to keep from the other cat shifter species. Mark realized a moment later that he shouldn't have been so surprised. His own Clan had many secrets, as well.

He bowed his head. "I'm not a mage," he replied, honestly.

"You may not be, but she is," Mitch nodded toward Shelly, who had a deer-in-the-headlights sort of expression on her face.

"Uh…" Shelly stammered a bit, but Mark couldn't help but come to her rescue.

"If she is, that's something that's only just come to light. Shelly grew up human. If she has mage blood, it's news to her," Mark told them.

"I grew up among humans," the Tig'Ren put in, patting Shelly's hand in a sympathetic way. "I've lived a normal human life most of the time, but I always knew I was a shifter. I had a firm foundation. I can't imagine what it must be like for you to have all of this happen to you at once."

"It's a bit much to take in. I only found out about shapeshifters a couple of days ago," Shelly admitted. "The sparky thing that happened yesterday was…" Shelly trailed off, seeming unable to complete her sentence.

"We were up at the caldera." Mark decided to come clean. If the tigers knew about volcanoes and the magic the way they claimed, they might just be the only people who could help. "Something happened, and red sparks came from Shelly's fingers. They seemed to be absorbed by the obsidian rock up there. I swear it looked and felt like the rock was welcoming the sparks."

Mitch eyed Shelly with a speculative glance. "You might just be a fire mage. In which case, you would be amply suited to commune with even a dormant volcano."

Shelly's eyes grew wide in a mix of denial and fear. Mark didn't fully understand why she was so afraid of the idea of magic. She'd seemed to handle the news about shifters pretty well, and her entire family line had worshipped the Goddess, just like him and his Clan, but ever since magic had become a topic of conversation, she'd been in denial. There was something more to it, he was sure, and he made a note to meet with her father at the earliest opportunity to see if he might know more.

The tiger royals didn't stay the night because, as Mark expected, they were on a tight schedule. Even stopping at the island for a few hours had set them behind, but if Mitch was to be believed—and Mark did believe him—the possibility of forming an alliance with the jaguar Clan was as important to Mitch as it was to Mark. The groundwork had been laid, and Mark expected good things to come of this first meeting. In fact, they'd already scheduled time to get together for a more in-depth discussion of business interests next week, when Mitch and Gina planned to be back in New York.

Tomorrow, he would go back with Shelly and arrange a meeting with her father, the elusive William Howell the Fourth. Before that, though, they had another night here on the island to enjoy.

This time, they ate dinner with the Clan. Everyone was welcoming and jovial. Those who had seen the tigers had been uniformly impressed by them, and word had gotten around that they had all parted on good terms. Things were looking up, and everyone knew it.

That, plus the Clan's reaction to Shelly—which was more positive than Mark could have hoped for—made for a raucous meal shared among friends. Mark and Shelly might be sitting in places of honor in the room—Mark couldn't quite get his people to give up that tradition—but the camaraderie was strong between them all. Mark wasn't one to stand on ceremony. He didn't style himself a monarch. He was just an Alpha who happened to have a lot more authority and recognition in the human world than most. That was all. He was responsible for his people, and he liked it that way.

He also liked the way they accepted Shelly. Though she was human, they didn't treat her any differently. They welcomed her as if she was already one of the family. It was his deepest desire to make her that in truth. As far as he was concerned, he was already committed. He just needed her to agree to be his mate. That was all that was needed among shifters, but he'd go further and take all the steps necessary to bind them legally together—in her world, and in his.

Besides, the society pages would pay well for pictures of their wedding. One of his people routinely brokered deals with various newspapers to get them *secret* photos. The photos weren't all that secret, but a calculated way for Mark to earn a little extra money for the Clan by bartering some of his unexpected celebrity.

He didn't really understand why ordinary humans wanted to follow his comings and goings so closely, but if people would pay him—through back channels, of course—for images of his public life, he didn't mind feeding the beast from time to time. Sometimes, he wondered what they'd pay if they knew he was a jaguar at heart, but shifters lived in secret for safety. It hadn't always been that way, but in this modern age, it was better to be prudent than dead.

At least by supplying the photos, he already knew what was in them. And the market for paparazzi was quelled. If the papers could get images of Mark anytime they wanted from an inside source, they wouldn't pay top dollar to stalkers with cameras. Win-win, as Shelly would have put it.

Conversation was lively, both at dinner and after. Mark and Shelly sat with a number of his closest friends, enjoying dessert and coffee for a couple of hours, until he noticed Shelly politely trying to hide a yawn. He didn't want her to be too tired. He had big plans for that night—the last they'd share on the island for a while.

He whisked her away from the gathering as nonchalantly as he could, taking her to his suite, not her guest room. When she didn't protest, he smiled. Oh, yes, he and his mate were definitely on the same page.

Shelly felt all tingly when Mark took her by the hand and led her up to what had to be his room in the mansion. It wasn't the biggest, nor the most luxurious. Actually, it was about the same as the guest room they'd given her down the hall, but it definitely had Mark's personal stamp on it.

He'd lifted her into his arms and carried her over the threshold, eliciting a gasp as he caught her off guard. The man made her breathless a lot—in a really good way.

There were mementoes of his youth displayed in a corner cabinet and photos of him and his friends hanging on the walls. The furniture was solid wood and sturdy. Oak, stained and polished to a loving luster. The fabrics were dark blues and hunter green with golden accents here and there. It almost had the look of a color scheme developed by a professional decorator, but she suspected Mark had chosen everything in here for himself. She got a quick look around the room before he started kissing her, and then, all thought fled as he lowered her to the big bed with the soft bedspread.

His kisses drugged her into wholehearted compliance with his every wish. The fact that he followed even her slightest direction made her happy too. When she tugged at his shirt, a moment later, it was gone, and she could place her hand directly on his solid, muscular chest. Mmm. He was a deliciously built specimen of manhood...shifter-hood...whatever. He was just lovely, whatever he was. The specifics didn't matter. He was her lover, and that was all there was to it.

When her hands went to his waistband, he lifted away momentarily, and when he came back, he was bare to her touch. Yes. Exactly what she wanted. She let herself explore, her hands finding all sorts of interesting things that had been hidden beneath his clothing. Especially a hard rod of iron covered in velvet heat that she wanted deep inside her as soon as they could manage.

While he'd undressed for her, he'd also been undressing her. She was as naked as he when he swept the bedspread aside, placing her squarely in the center of the enormous bed. This bed had been built with someone Mark's size in mind, but it dwarfed Shelly a bit. No matter. There would be plenty of room for both of them to be comfortable, which was the important thing.

He came down over her, but he was lower on the bed than she'd expected. When he lifted one of her feet to his shoulder and began nibbling on the inside of her leg, she giggled. When he moved lower to lick the back of her knee, she trembled in reaction. And when he moved to her thighs, she held her breath.

Was he going to…? Oh, yes. Yes, he was.

She just about lost her mind when his tongue reached out and licked her clit, exploring and laving, arousing and electrifying. Then, his lips moved on her, giving her the most intimate of kisses, his talented tongue invading and retreating, driving her into blissful delirium.

She couldn't take much of that treatment and shuddered, coming hard against his mouth. She could feel him smile against her most sensitive skin and felt the purr of his satisfaction rumbling through his chest as he rose to settle more fully over her limp body.

She felt boneless. Sated for the moment but still interested in what he had to offer.

When he rolled her onto her side, she went with him, unsure where he was leading but willing to follow. He hadn't steered her wrong yet, and her famous instincts said she could trust him in all things. *All* things.

He positioned himself behind her and lifted her top leg back and over his thigh. It was a bit awkward at first, but she was intrigued by what he evidently had in mind.

He slid into her from behind. It was a shallow penetration, but the position made it tighter than she'd expected, and new sensations flooded her body, making it perk up instantly in interest. Forget the lovely climax he'd just given her. She was greedy for more.

As he moved, she adjusted to the odd angles, shifting into each thrust as he supported her, his big hands positioned at her hip and around her midsection. She felt the tempered strength in his fingers, his excitement in the tremble and strain of his muscles. He pushed her ever onward toward another magnificent climax, and she went willingly, wanting him with her, this time, when she blew.

She strained backward against him, and they came together in harsh, fast motions that grew in intensity until the pressure was off the charts. She screamed his name as she climaxed, feeling his fingers dig into her body in a way that might've been painful at any other time, but felt amazing in the here and now.

She flew to the moon, but he wasn't done. He kept moving throughout, pushing her higher, harder, faster, deeper, until she reached the nearest star and exploded for a second time. Then, he did something—shifted her leg, or his, or something she couldn't see behind her back—and she started climbing again. She'd never experienced anything like this before. Multiple orgasms. Two very lame words that stood for one of the most amazing experiences of her life.

Then, Mark moved his hand from her hip down to the apex of her thighs, and she sucked in a breath. His finger zeroed in on her clit, and she went supernova this time, out among the galaxies, firing the stars and suns.

In the real world, sparks flew around them, but she was lost to reality for a few minutes while her spirit flew.

When she came back to earth, she was relieved to note that she hadn't actually burned anything. Her sparks had been a visual show only. She thought. She blinked her eyes open to find Mark staring at her. He'd positioned them facing each other, both reclining in his big bed, on their sides.

"Did you see the sparks?" she whispered, her brain not really fully functioning just yet.

He brought one of her hands to his lips. "Saw them and felt them. They energized me and gave me strength I didn't know I had."

"Really?" she squeaked, surprised.

"Really." He nodded, sucking one of her fingers into his mouth and making her gasp.

"Did they burn?" Her voice was breathless, but whether from the exertion they'd just completed or the way his tongue was dueling with her finger, she couldn't tell. Was it possible she could become aroused again so soon? Could he?

She looked downward at his body and realized he could, indeed. Wow. Perhaps that was another benefit of being a shifter. Or maybe that virility was something special to just Mark, himself. Either way, she was a lucky, lucky girl.

"It tickled," he said, letting go of her finger so he could speak. "I thought, at first, it might cause a fire in the room, but I didn't really care at that point. As it turned out, the sparks were showy but not damaging. They were sort of little zaps of energy against my skin that sent my arousal higher. Quite the talent there, my little love," he complimented her, and for some reason, she blushed.

"I didn't know," she stammered, embarrassed for some reason.

"I know, *querida*," he whispered, drawing her close to kiss her sweetly. "Rest now. I can give you a few minutes before I need you again. You are a fire in my veins that will never be quenched."

That sounded serious, but she was too confused by everything that had just happened, and still a little muddled from the amazing multiple orgasms she had experienced to really think about it. There would be time to think later. Judging by the way he was stroking her skin...*much* later.

CHAPTER 11

Shelly was sad to leave the island the next morning. She had only been there for two days, but she felt connected…somehow…to the place. She could very easily be seduced by the setting into doing anything Mark asked, without thinking things all the way through. Thinking over every decision was her *thing*.

Some people took leaps of faith. Shelly definitely looked a few times and inspected every angle before she leapt anywhere. She had a cautious nature that made her good at her profession, but when faced with a situation like the one she was in right now with Mark, her mind became a muddle of confusion. She needed some space to sit quietly and think things through.

Beautiful as it was, she knew she wouldn't get the distance or perspective she needed on the island. No, she had to be away from this tropical paradise, back in her own element. In her own house. The space she had claimed just for herself, with all her comfortable objects and possessions around her.

Only then could she find the calm center of the whirlwind she'd been riding since that dinner party where Mark had been targeted for assassination. It seems like months ago now, and it had only been a couple of days. Time was skewed. That was another thing she had to sit down and think about. Everything had happened so fast. She couldn't keep up.

Once she was home, working in her own studio, in familiar surroundings, she would be able to regain her balance. At least, that was the plan. A small part of her worried that something about this trip, and Mark, had changed her forever. She couldn't pinpoint exactly what had happened, but she thought she knew when.

It had been when they made love in the caldera of the volcano. Something had definitely happened then. She still wasn't sure what to call it, or what the implications for the future might be. Mark kept insisting she was somehow magical, but that couldn't be right. Could it?

"I can't be seen with you just yet," Mark explained as they flew back toward her home on the mainland in a different luxury jet from the one they'd arrived in. How many of these things did he own? "We're going to take extra precautions, just in case."

She grew concerned at his worried expression. Was there a reason to fear? Or… She hated to think this… But was this the big brush off? Had the playboy billionaire gotten what he wanted and now wasn't interested anymore?

Shelly had a hard time believing that, but some niggling echo of doubt wouldn't let the thought go. She hadn't had a lot of experience with men—and certainly not those in Mark's circles. She was no supermodel. No foreign beauty who would do anything for a rich man who paid her bills. She was just a good architect from a formerly well-to-do family. Not much of a catch, really, for a man who could have anything—or any*one*—he wanted.

Self-doubt was a terrible thing, but Shelly was as susceptible to it as anyone else. Maybe even more, since she and her father had never had a truly close relationship. After her mother died, she had wanted to reach out to him, but he had been dealing with his own grief. Even though her father still lived and they saw each other often at society functions and the obligatory celebrations and holidays, they weren't really that close. Shelly had tried repeatedly to get to know her dad better, but he was a very controlled sort of man.

She knew he loved her, of course, but he wasn't excessively demonstrative. They did have a good working relationship, though. He'd often send her invitations—like the one to the dinner where she'd encountered Mark—that he thought would help her network for her architectural business. He thought about her and was helpful, but he wasn't a doting father by any stretch of the imagination.

It had been hard not to feel rejected on occasion when she'd tried to deepen the relationship and her father had backed off.

Was Mark now rejecting her too? She didn't want to believe it, but it just might be true.

Oh, Goddess, what was she going to do?

Right then, she realized she was already in way over her head with this man. She'd been so cautious, but it had all been for naught. Mark had cast the spell, and she'd fallen. Head over heels, she'd fallen.

Mark didn't like the look on Shelly's face, but he figured she would forgive him once she realized he had other plans in mind to circumvent any possible surveillance. He'd had his people watching her house while they'd been on the island. His people had also been busy installing state-of-the-art security hardware on her land. He held the passwords and all the control. Nobody but he—and a few trusted Clan members—could get to her by conventional means now. Not without tripping an alarm. And Mark had made damned sure it would be jaguars answering that alarm, if it ever came. If not him, personally, then one of his trusted Clan members.

Shelly was one of them now, and jaguars took care of their own. She may not be a shifter, but she was his mate, and after the past two days, the heart of the Clan was well on their way to accepting her. Now if he could just convince her.

"I've had some security measures added to your property. Nothing you'll see—or at least you shouldn't. It's all well hidden and camouflaged, and the signals go directly to my people," he told her. Maybe she'd see his need to protect her as the declaration it really was.

"You didn't have to do that," she protested, but her expression had changed from one of doubt and worry to something more thoughtful. Good.

"It's my pleasure to look after you," he told her, bringing her hand to his lips because he just couldn't help himself. He had to touch her. To kiss her. To remind her that she was his. Even if she hadn't agreed to that just yet. "I'll come to you tonight, if at all possible. First, I have a few things I need to put in place, but when it's safe, I will come to you, no matter where you are, no matter the time."

He kissed her fingertips, one at a time. Those magical little digits that had sparked the heart of a dormant volcano. How she could continue in the belief that she had no magic was incredible to him. How could she not see it?

But the look of doubt had disappeared from her eyes now, which gratified him. He didn't want her to worry about anything. Especially not his commitment to her. Ever.

He knew, of course, that such things took time among humans. Magical as she was, she still believed she was completely human—and had grown up with human standards. He had to be patient. The Goddess was making him work for this, it was true, but he wouldn't be any kind of an Alpha if he couldn't appreciate a challenge.

Mark let Shelly go with great reluctance when they landed on the mainland an hour later. He'd spent the flight talking with her in low, intimate tones, when he would much rather have been doing something *a lot more* intimate than merely talking. Joining the Mile High Club with her was definitely on his to-do list, but not today. Not in this particular plane, which had no private sleeping compartment.

Another one of their jets did, and he hoped to take her with him some place suitably distant enough that they would have sufficient time to put that big bed to good use. But that was a plan for another day. Today, he had to check in with the security team watching her house and get updates from a number of his subordinates, as well as the Midtown wolf Pack, who had been helping. There was work to do, and plenty of it.

Mark hit the ground running and didn't slow down for anything. The faster he got his work done, the sooner he could sneak into Shelly's house and make love with her. With incentive like that, he couldn't fail.

Work done for the day, Mark was already in his car—a sleek Italian sports car he liked to take out on long drives—when his cell phone rang. It was the Midtown Pack Alpha, relaying a message from his brother, who had been helping with surveillance on Shelly's home, along with a few other wolves. It was a good trade—the younger brother got real-world experience and training from some of Mark's senior people, and the jaguars got extra manpower from a local source, with potentially different local sources of intel.

Cassius reported a sighting of one of the cars they had been on the lookout for. They had a short list of persons of interest headed by the jackass who had accosted Shelly in the elevator of the hotel. *Venifucus* agent Antony Mason had three vehicles that they knew of, and all three were on a watch list for those stationed around Shelly's home.

Mason reportedly lived in New Jersey, so seeing one of his vehicles in Shelly's neighborhood was highly suspect. There were few legitimate reasons for him to be there. Especially at this time of night.

It was well after midnight, with few cars on the road, so Mark felt no trepidation in flooring the gas pedal and making for Shelly's as quickly as possible. He could feel it now. The closer he got to her place, the more something felt…not right. Threatening.

A gathering gloom in the night made him slow down. His headlights cut a path through the dark miasma like a spoon sliding through thick soup. Pea soup fog was something Northeasterners experienced every once in awhile, but this was dark, not the white of fog. His car's headlights weren't reflected off water vapor; instead, they were swallowed up by the darkness itself.

This could not be good.

Mark tried dialing every number he had for Shelly, but nothing went through. Then, he tried to get in touch with his security detail around her house. Same problem. They'd been cut off.

Mark called the Midtown Alpha back and asked for backup to be sent, but he had the sinking feeling they wouldn't get there in time. This would be up to whoever was already there, and Mark alone was the cavalry.

Goddess help them all.

*

Shelly shivered, pulling her cardigan closer around her body and rubbing her upper arms. She was up late, which wasn't abnormal for her when she really got immersed in a project. Seeing the island had been inspirational in so many ways. Ideas were sparking in her mind, and she knew she would stay up as long as she could to get as many of them down on paper as possible.

There was so much to be done there. So much they could do with that beautiful landscape and magical location. She'd already fleshed out the sketches she'd made for the community center. She was getting into the nitty-gritty details of plumbing, electrical, and room layouts now. One of her favorite parts of any job. This was the stage where she could imagine people living in and using the fixtures and furniture she made room for in her designs. It was sort of like playing with an imaginary dollhouse on paper that would, someday, become real. Full-scale.

She'd always thought that was a lot of fun. How many people got to see their dreams become reality in such a tangible way?

But something had interrupted her train of thought. She'd

been sitting at her drafting table, working the old-fashioned way with pencil and paper, rulers and grids, but something had disturbed her. She'd stood, felt the cold and checked the thermostat, but unless it was reading incorrectly, the house was at a comfortable seventy-two degrees Fahrenheit. They way she always kept it.

So then, why was she cold?

She glanced out the window then looked again. The garden was dark. Completely dark in a way that wasn't normal. Shelly scowled. What was going on out there? Had they forecast fog? But that didn't look like fog…

Her hands started to tingle, and a buzzing sound echoed through the house. Only the sound wasn't registering in her ears, but in her mind. It was a silent hum that felt like a billion angry wasps droning around her head. What the…?

A flash of sickly green roiled through the black outside like an oil slick. Only, this wasn't even remotely pretty. It was putrid. The buzzing intensified as she watched the tendril of green ooze approach her home.

As she watched it get closer and closer, it suddenly stopped. Halted, as if it had run into a brick wall, about five feet from her house. She watched as it spread outward and then upward, seeking a break in the invisible shield that, somehow, was protecting her home from…whatever this was.

It streaked upward, right past the window through which she was looking. She leaned closer to see it go up past the rooftop then curve overhead, as if there was a dome over her house. What in the world?

Movement from the driveway caught her eye. Shelly looked down to see the man from the elevator stepping out of the darkness. It seemed to be coming from him, somehow. Accepting him. Liking the feel of him. That alone made her feel sick to her stomach. There was something very wrong with that blackness. Something disgusting about it. Something…evil.

Antony, she remembered. He'd said his name was Antony

Mason. But what in the world was he doing here? Had he been watching for her? Waiting for her to return? And why?

She had a sinking feeling she knew why. He was after Mark. He'd been way too interested in the events of that night in Manhattan. He'd been friendly with the shooter, no matter that he claimed later not to be. This man was a liar. And that was the least of his sins, she was sure.

How she knew that, she didn't fully understand, but she felt the truth of it in her heart. The buzzing increased again as he strode through the black wrongness that seemed to welcome him. He walked right up to her front door—or as close as he could get to it, which looked like that same five-foot barrier that the green goo had faced.

He stood there, looking at the remnants of the green plasma, now dissipating as it swirled harmlessly against whatever that shield was around her house. Was that something Mark's people had put in place? She'd have to ask him.

Antony lifted one hand to try to touch the barrier, but it gave him a sizzling white shock of mini-lightning that had him pulling his hand back with a curse. Whatever it was, the barrier had stopped this Antony guy in his tracks. He had his hands on his hips, staring at it, and his face was contorted with anger.

"You will not keep me out, mistress of the cat," he spat, raising his gaze to meet hers as she gasped in shock. That he'd known exactly where she was standing creeped her out.

"Go away," she shouted, unsure if he could even hear her through the glass, but needing to say something.

"I'm not going anywhere without your blood, cat-whore!" he said in a voice that somehow carried up to her window and through it to reach her ears. Or maybe it was buzzing in her mind the way that…energy…or whatever it was, had done.

"Why?" she whispered, wanting to know what fueled the rage she saw on Antony's face. "Why Mark? Why are you doing this?"

"That fucking cat stands in the way of my plans and my promotion within the ranks of the *Venifucus*. Kill him and I move up to stand at the foot of the altar to the *Mater Priori*, Elspeth, the Destroyer of Worlds." Antony practically salivated as he said the words, then seemed to sober. "This was the task I was given. Kill the jaguar, and my future is assured," he said as if repeating a sick and twisted mantra.

"Never," Shelly said, not sure how or if Antony could hear her, but it had to be said. The world could no longer exist without Mark in it. At least not for her.

The droning sound in the back of her mind rose as Antony backed up a few paces then held out both arms in front of him, and that green plasma shot from both of his hands. It was a concentrated attack on the barrier only a few feet away. The green was way more intense this time. Bright, sickly green that made her want to puke.

The feel of it against her home—for, she realized, she could feel the attack inside her own body in some strange sort of way—made her feel sick. And then, it made her angry. So angry, she marched down the stairs and threw open the front door before she even knew what she was doing.

"Stop!" she screamed at Antony, lifting her own hands and letting her rage at his attack pour out. How dare he come here and try to hurt her? How dare he target Mark for death? How dare he attack her in her own territory? On her own ground? Outrage filled her and roiled in her blood.

Those red sparks she had seen first on the island were back, and there was no doubt, this time, that they came directly from her. Mark wasn't around. She couldn't explain away the magic as being some kind of byproduct of his presence. No, this was all on her. All *from* her. She would own it, and she would control it. And she would use it to defend her home in any way possible.

Much to her surprise, Antony flew back, into the trees across the width of her driveway. As he disappeared into the darkness, she heard him scream, followed by wet crunching sounds that made her wince.

Had she really just done that? Had she propelled a grown man with obvious magical power away from her house with only those innocent-looking red sparks? Shelly looked down at her hands, expecting to see burns, but she was whole, untouched. If she hadn't just witnessed it herself, she wouldn't really believe it.

The sickly black receded as quickly as it had rolled in, and the sickly green plasma was nowhere to be seen when a sleek black jaguar prowled out of the cleansing mist of a normal fog that lay delicately in the trees and on her driveway. It was as if the evil had been swept away by a cleansing breath of fog.

She knew the jaguar. It was Mark.

Maybe those sparks hadn't been hers, after all?

No. There was no way she could weasel her way out of this one. She had to take ownership of the strange magic that seemed to have taken up residence in her soul. She had no doubt in her mind that exposure to Mark, and his people, had brought on this strange magic, but she also felt like it was here to stay. Once awakened, there was no stuffing this genie back in its bottle.

She liked the thought of that. But she wasn't sure if they were totally out of danger yet. Antony had disappeared into the trees, and she had a good idea what had happened to him after that, considering Mark's presence. Had Antony come alone? Or did he have friends waiting in the wings?

Shelly sent out her senses in search. She didn't think the fog would come in and the darkness recede if they were still in danger, but Mark looked extra vigilant as he prowled up to the barrier that still seemed to be in place. He sniffed at it, even tested it with one paw. It didn't reject him like it had Antony, but it also didn't let him in.

"Is it safe?" she whispered to Mark, so close, yet so far away. She suspected that, if she wanted to cross the barrier, she could, but she wasn't sure if she would be able to come back.

Mark shifted shape in a shower of dark sparkles. One

minute, he was a cat. The next, he was a very handsome, very naked man.

"Better stay behind the ward for now," he told her. "We took some casualties from the fog and the plasma. I have backup on the way, but we're going to be busy out here for a little while."

"Casualties?" She gulped. "Is everyone still alive?" Dear Goddess, she hoped nobody had paid the ultimate price to protect her.

"All alive on our side, and it looks like it'll stay that way. How about you? Are you okay?" His gaze spoke of his concern, and she felt tears well up behind her eyes.

She'd been so strong up to this point. She wouldn't weaken now. Not when Mark had others to see to. He needed her to be strong. She knew that. She could fall apart later. When it was just them, alone together.

"I'm fine. You probably saw... He never even got close to the house. This barrier thing sprung up out of nowhere and encapsulated the whole structure. Did your people do this?" She looked up at the night sky, once again visible now that the inky blackness Antony had spawned was gone. Stars sparkled down on them, and a light layer of fog rolled around their ankles.

"No, *querida*, that was already here. It is something we call a ward. It's a magical thing created by mages, not usually shifters, and certainly none of the people I left here have this kind of power. Someone else is protecting you." His gaze turned concerned.

"Seriously?" Shelly couldn't think who could have possibly put such a thing around her house without her knowing it.

"Do you know any magic users? Mages? Witches? Wizards?" His lopsided smile was both amused and sexy as hell. Damn, she wanted to touch those broad shoulders.

"Um...none of the above. As far as I know." Just then, her telephone started ringing in the house. It was the landline.

"Your phone lines weren't working before," Mark offered.

"None of them?" She'd had her cell phone charging on

the desk next to her while she worked and hadn't heard a single beep from it all night long.

"Not a one. I couldn't reach you or any of my people. You'd better go see who that is," he told her gently. "I'm going to be out in the woods for a bit. Meet you back here in fifteen minutes?"

"Deal." He turned away, and the phone was still ringing, but she had to say something. "And Mark?" He turned back to meet her gaze. "Thank you." She tried to put everything she was feeling into those two simple words.

He nodded, and she thought he probably understood. He'd helped save her life tonight. She honestly didn't know how she would have handled Antony alone. She might've been able to repulse him with her sparks, but that might have just been beginner's luck. Mark had done the heavy lifting.

She had a pretty good idea that he'd just killed to save her, and far from being repulsed by the idea, she was more thankful than she could express. He'd proven that he would protect her. He'd put himself on the line for her. To Shelly, there was no greater declaration than that.

A shower of dark sparkles against the fog and Mark was back to his black panther form. He stalked into the woods, disappearing from sight between one moment and the next. He was really good at that stealth stuff.

Shelly raced back into the house to pick up the landline that was still ringing.

"Hello?" She might've sounded a little out of breath, but it didn't matter. Nobody should be calling her this late at night.

CHAPTER 12

"Shelly, honey, is everything all right?"

It was her father's voice. Someone she never would have expected to call her so late—or after such an event. Had he known? Was he somehow watching her house?

"All good here, Dad. How are you?" she asked, not really sure how to come out and ask him what she really wanted to know. Had *he* placed—or hired someone to place—the *ward*, as Mark had called it? No. It was too ridiculous to contemplate. Then again... "It's kind of late for you to be calling. What's the matter?"

"You should probably be telling me that, don't you think?" A heavy sigh came over the line. "Something happened at your house tonight, didn't it?"

"Uh...yeah...something. How did you know?" She toyed with a loose tendril of her hair while she talked to him, feeling like a child all over again. A child who had never quite known what he wanted her to say.

"Maybe you'd better tell me what you saw first," he backpedalled, slipping into a quieter tone meant to coax her to talk. She remembered that well from her childhood, but she didn't mind. She loved her father, even if she'd never fully understood him.

She blew out a frustrated breath. "You'd never believe it in a million years."

"Try me," he replied gently. "But first, you should know two things. One—your landline is totally secure. Nobody can eavesdrop on our conversation through conventional means. And two—I've been waiting for this day for a long time."

"It's the middle of the night." She said literally the first thing that popped into her mind. Her father's warm chuckle on the other end of the line touched a chord inside her as she sat down on the sofa and tried to figure out how to describe what had just happened.

"Start at the beginning. That always works best," her father encouraged.

"Well, I was working up in my studio when I looked out the window. No, wait, there was this chill and then a buzzing sound in my head." She paused, trying to recall the exact sequence of events.

Over the next five minutes, she managed to tell him about everything that had happened up to the point where Mark had emerged from the woods and onto her driveway. Then, she faltered. How to explain Mark? Could she even talk about his presence here? His secret was sacrosanct. It was up to him to decide who knew about him and his people. It was not her secret to share. She couldn't make that decision.

But it was okay. Her father picked up the thread of the conversation when her story petered out. He'd been silent the whole time, but it was an encouraging sort of silence, not a condemning one.

She hoped.

"You saw the ward?" her father asked finally, making her question her perception of reality.

That question, right there, indicated he not only knew about the magic shield around her house, but that he knew a lot more about magic than she ever would have suspected. Dear Goddess! *He knows about magic?*

"I saw the ward," she said mechanically, stunned by this entire exchange.

"And you shot sparks out of your fingers? Enough to hurl

him across the driveway and into the trees?" Her father's voice continued in that patient, encouraging tone.

She nodded, even though he couldn't see her. "Yeah, I did, Dad."

"Oh, Shelly, I'm so proud of you."

Had his voice just cracked with emotion? Sweet Mother of All. *What* was happening here?

"I'm getting in the car, and I'll be right there. Watch for me. It'll take about fifteen minutes, and then, we'll talk, okay? Just hold on for another fifteen minutes and don't step beyond the ward. There might still be danger out there, lurking in the trees."

"Uh, Dad?" How to explain Mark and his friends prowling in the woods? It was probably okay to at least mention their presence. He'd see them anyway when he got here. Probably.

"Yes, honey?" She could hear him moving around as if he was getting into the car. He must be on his cell.

"There are some people in the yard around my house, but they're friends. I met someone last week at that fundraiser, and he and I have been working together. He stationed some of his friends around my house, to sort of keep an eye on things after…well, after what happened at the dinner."

"You mean the dinner where some jackass took a shot at Mark Pepard?"

Her father might not have as much money as he used to, but he still kept up with current events in their social circles. Plus, that had been front page news, though her involvement had been kept mercifully out of the papers. Probably thanks to Mark, she realized now.

"Yeah. Mark asked me to design some structures for a project he's involved in. We've been working together pretty closely for the past couple of days."

"Mark Pepard?" Her father's voice took on a serious, low tone. "Honey, do you know what he is?"

"Um…"

"Oh, dear Goddess," her father breathed over the line. He paused then seemed to gather himself. "Is he there now?"

"Uh…yeah." She felt safe to say that much, though it certainly sounded like her father knew exactly who and what Mark was. How in the world…?

"Okay. Sit tight. I'm on my way," her father told her. She could hear his car moving in the background. He was already driving. "Nobody will be able to cross the ward until I reset it. Don't let him try."

"He did, but it didn't shock him. It just didn't let him in," she told her dad.

"Really?" Now, her father sounded intrigued. "Hmm. Well, that's a good sign. You said there were more of his people out there with him?"

"Yeah, and some local…um…friends, who've been supplementing his security team. They've been here a couple of days." She could still hardly believe this conversation. Not only did her dad know about magic, but he seemed to know about *Mark*.

"Good gracious. What in the world did you get mixed up in?" He seemed almost as if he was talking to himself, so she didn't answer. "Never mind. I'll be there in a few minutes and we can sort this all out. Shelly, did Pepard see the sparks? Did he see you use your magic?"

"Yeah, Dad. He saw." If Mark hadn't seen it this time, he'd certainly gotten a good view on the island. Mark had been the one to recognize the magic for what it was, while she'd still been in denial.

Her father sighed again. "I guess it couldn't be helped. No matter. Pepard has enough secrets of his own. I doubt he'll be spilling yours to all and sundry."

"No, Dad. He wouldn't do that," she felt compelled to defend him.

"Oh, bright Lady, you're not *involved* with him, are you?"

Shelly cringed. She wasn't sure what her dad was going to say to this, but she had to tell him the truth.

"Um… Yeah, I guess you could say we're involved."

"Dear, oh, dear." That was an expression her mother used to use. To hear her father say, it now brought back memories.

133

"Do you know if he's serious?"

"Yeah, I think he is. But I guess you can talk to him when you get here. He's outside again. I'm going to walk to the door and let him know you're coming so he can tell his guys to expect you, okay?" Shelly got up and took the phone with her to the door.

Mark had reappeared at the barrier, buttoning the shirt he must've discarded in a hurry when he'd seen she needed help. He was dressed again in no time, and she was glad he would be presentable when her father arrived. The situation was complicated enough.

"Hold on for a minute, Dad," she told her father, then leaned out the door to talk to Mark. "My dad is on his way in. You might want to tell your friends. He's probably driving an old silver Rolls. He says he will reset the ward when he gets here but that I shouldn't step outside the boundary until everything is secure." She could hardly believe she was having this conversation—talking about magic as if she was discussing the latest news. Could her life get any weirder?

Mark's eyebrows rose as she delivered that last bit. Yeah, he'd figured it out. Her dad knew about magic.

"Sounds like we'll all have a lot to discuss," was Mark's only comment.

William Howell the Fourth was nothing like Mark had expected. If he'd had the time or inclination to read the detailed dossier he was certain his people had put together on the entire Howell family, complete with photos, he probably would have been better prepared. Mark had wanted to learn about his mate and her family more naturally, through interaction.

Of course, circumstances had conspired against his plan, and events had accelerated the natural progression. The man who drove up in a vintage Rolls looked a lot younger than Mark had anticipated. He gave the appearance of being a much older brother, not the father with the rather intimidating name.

He stepped out of the Rolls easily, his gait that of a much younger man. He had energy to spare, it seemed. And the warning twinkle in his eye as their gazes met wasn't entirely friendly. Oh, yeah. There was the protective dad side, for sure.

Mark met him in the driveway, holding out a hand in greeting. "You must be Mr. Howell. I'm Mark Pepard."

"Call me Bill," Shelly's father said in a firm voice as their hands met. And there it was. The telltale tingle of magic.

Mark tilted his head in an inquisitive motion but said nothing about the little spark that had just passed between their hands. "Please call me Mark," he said, instead, hoping to keep this first encounter with his mate's father on friendly footing.

Bill stepped back and looked at the house. Shelly stood in the entry, and he winked at her, Mark saw. The man had very expressive sparkling blue eyes. He saw now where Shelly got at least part of her good looks from.

"Stay right where you are, sweet pea," Bill told Shelly. "This won't take but a moment."

And with that, he lifted both hands in the air and chanted a few words under his breath that even Mark with his shifter hearing couldn't distinguish. He felt the rising magic, though. It was powerful and intense.

As fast as it rose, it fell again, as if the invisible dome that had encircled the house suddenly rose and collapsed into a tiny circle in the ground around the perimeter of the structure. Son of a... Mark realized the ward had been there all along. Shelly's dad had been looking out for her, and her property, even though she didn't know anything about magic.

For Mark was still sure Shelly hadn't been faking. She wasn't some witch in hiding. She had truly not known about shifters or magic, or anything remotely paranormal before their first encounter.

Her father now... He was another story.

"Very neat work," Mark commented as Bill dropped his hands back to his sides. He nodded in acknowledgement of the compliment.

"Shall we adjourn to the living room?" Bill invited, as if he was hosting this little party.

Mark motioned for him to go first, which he did, while Mark gave an imperceptible hand signal to his team. They would be on watch. Most of them were okay, though drained. The magic had bound them, and their struggles against it had taken a lot out of them all, but they'd be okay until the werewolves he'd asked for backup arrived. They'd be here any minute, and then, there would be fresh troops in the woods, watching the house.

Bill walked right up to his daughter and gave her a big hug before they said anything to each other. Mark admired the deep emotion in the gesture. It was clear they cared for one another. Good. That was healthy. He'd been afraid that the father had kept Shelly in the dark all these years because they didn't get along, but it looked to be the opposite.

After all, he'd come running at the first sign of trouble. Bill, so far, impressed Mark as a good dad.

When the hug ended, Shelly turned and let them into the house, heading straight for the living room. She sat on the couch, and her astute father sat opposite in a wing chair, leaving the spot next to her open for Mark to take…if he dared. He didn't back down from the challenge. He sat, a small declaration of intent.

"First of all, let me say how happy I am to finally be able to share the wider world with you, Shelly," her father said before anyone else could speak.

"Why didn't you before? Why did you keep me in the dark my whole life?" Shelly sounded hurt, as she probably should be. Mark wanted to know the answer to that question, as well. Everything else could wait until she got that answer.

Bill sighed elegantly. "The Howells have a long tradition of magic, going back thousands of years. Occasionally, in our family history, a child is born with no magic. They were called *latent* by one of our ancestors in the family chronicles, because no Howell can be completely without magic. It's part of our

DNA. But, as I said, there are historical accounts of the occasional latent Howell. In times past, there were enough Howells to keep those few safe, but now, it's you and me, sweet pea, and since your mother's death, I've always feared I wouldn't be able to keep you safe. All I ever wanted was to keep my precious daughter away from those who would use her against me. I've been nearly bankrupting myself all these years trying to keep you safe, Shelly."

"So, that's why…" Shelly whispered.

"I didn't *want* to drive a wedge between us, my dear. It was necessary to keep a certain distance so my enemies wouldn't see you as too tempting a target. All the same, I put whatever protections I could around you at all times. Hence, the ward on your house." He nodded toward the window. "You have no idea how relieved I am that you're all right."

"Dad, that ward thing… That was awesome. It protected me and the house completely," Shelly enthused.

"I'm glad. That was my intent. I have spent years learning ward-craft, and that was some of my finest work, if I do say so myself, though it hadn't been fully tested until tonight," Bill admitted.

Mark's ears perked up. "*Fully* tested? You mean it's been triggered before?"

Bill's eyes shuttered. "On occasion, a few of my more perceptive enemies have tried small forays to test my mettle. They all failed."

"And are all dead, I presume?" Mark asked the harsh question, hoping to evoke a response. What he got in return was everything he had hoped for. Bill's blue eyes went steely.

"Of course. Magic users don't screw around. You're either good or bad, and there is no in between. The Howells have always stood on the side of Light. We are sworn to the Goddess, through and through. Any agent of evil who threatens me or mine is fair game. Now, tell me, Alpha, which side does the jaguar stand on?"

Mark reared back, unable to hide his reaction. The jaguars were among the most secretive of shifters. Only the *pantera noir* were better at hiding in plain sight than he was. Or so he'd thought. Obviously, this mage had better sources of intel than Mark had credited.

"I, and my Clan, are sworn to the Light of the Mother of All," Mark answered finally, deciding on the direct approach. Who knew how Howell would react to any attempt at subterfuge when his beloved daughter's destiny was in question.

"Good. Good." Howell was all smiles as he relaxed fractionally. Mark noticed that quick unclenching of muscles and wondered what the man would have done if Mark had said something else. "I like what I'm hearing. And I must thank you for watching over my daughter. The ward was designed to alert me about trouble, with the idea that I could race right over and deal with it. I assume you've…dealt with the problem already?" Now those blue eyes were coaxing, as if he already knew or suspected the answer but wanted official confirmation.

"With tooth and claw," Mark confirmed, nodding gravely. The green plasma mage had tasted sickly. Evil.

"I would like to examine any…uh…remains, if possible," Bill asked politely.

Mark nodded. "That can be arranged. He disabled a number of my people with the dark fog, and I have backup already on the way. In fact, they should be here by now. My folk haven't done anything with the remains yet but guard them. We're stretched too thin for comfort until the cavalry arrives."

"Understood," Bill replied quickly, with an accommodating demeanor. "Perhaps, if possible then, I might get a look *in situ*, as it were." The older man rose fluidly from his wing chair and headed for the door. "I'll be back in a few minutes."

"My people saw you arrive," Mark called after him. "They'll stay out of your way."

"Of course they will, dear boy," Bill said on his way out, almost smiling.

Mark's eyebrows rose, then he looked at Shelly's equally stunned face. "He's got brass ones, your father, if you'll pardon the expression."

Shelly laughed out loud. "He always has. Nobody gets in his way, and if they try, he merely charms them away. He's always had that magic touch." She sat back on the couch, staring straight ahead. "Huh." Shaking her head, she turned to look at him. "I guess it really was magic, after all."

"I can't believe he was able to keep you in the dark all these years about your family history." Mark slid one arm around her shoulders and leaned back, content just to have her near.

"Neither can I. Though..." She squirmed closer into his embrace, and his inner cat purred. "Now that I understand a little more, I think I might've seen the signs occasionally. He had weird friends when I was little. Flamboyant old women who wore turbans and—"

"Now, don't speak ill of the dead, Shelly, or your great aunties might just come back from the next realm to haunt you. It's been known to happen in our family on rare occasions." Her father walked back into the room, adjusting his shirtsleeve, urbane and collected, even after seeing what Mark had done to the bastard who had dared to attack his mate. The cat had reveled in ripping him apart.

"Aunt Bernie and Auntie Francine!" Shelly sat upright, surprise on her face. "I remember them now. I was really little when they stopped coming around. They used to bring me treats from their travels. Sweet candies from around the world. What happened to them? I guess I didn't realize they were dead."

"It happened right around the time your dear mother was taken from us," her father said in a solemn tone. "Both of my father's sisters were killed in what was later described as a ferocious magical battle in which the side of Light was woefully underrepresented. Many good people died that day in the ongoing war between good and evil."

"I'm sorry. I didn't know," Shelly said, her face reflecting her sorrow.

"They were the last of us, except for you and me, Shelly. We're the bitter end of a thousand year magical line." He retook his seat on the wing chair. "I feared it would end with me, but now, it looks like you have finally come into your birthright, so perhaps the name will disappear, but the magic will live on." He sighed dramatically. "Very thorough job on the enemy, by the way, Mark. Well done." He looked directly at Mark. "You may want to warn your people and their backup to steer clear of the remains, though. They will require special handling. This man was one nasty piece of work, whoever he was."

"You didn't recognize him then?" Mark asked.

"Never seen him before. What can you tell me about him?" Bill was all business now.

"He seems to have been an associate of the man who tried to shoot me the other day. Because your daughter had coincidentally shared a cab with the man from the hotel to the venue, she was dragged in for questioning by my security. Once I realized she had nothing to do with the assassination attempt, I sent her on her way, but not before setting up surveillance, just in case."

"You also requested a meeting with me the next day, as I recall," Shelly put in with a smile, reaching out to take his hand in her. His inner cat wanted to pounce on her in happiness. She was staking a claim—a subtle one, but still a claim—in front of her father. Nice.

"As it turned out, I'm glad I took the precaution of calling in help from the Midtown wolf Pack. They were able to help Shelly when the mage confronted her in the hotel hallway and then followed her into the elevator."

"What did he want?" Bill asked Shelly directly.

"He was asking about his friend. The guy who had taken a shot at Mark. I told him I didn't know the man and basically told him to get lost, but he was very insistent. Actually, he was a little scary there toward the end, but then, the hotel staff—who I now assume were Mark's people or allies—

stepped in and breezed me out of there." Shelly frowned. "His name was Anthony Mason. He told me that at the hotel. But tonight he said some things…"

"He spoke to you?" Mark asked, his inner cat wanting to pounce on any information that might help him keep his mate safe.

"I was up in my studio and he walked right up to the ward. I didn't think he saw me, but he did. He looked right at me as he told me he had been given the task of killing you, Mark, by someone he called the Destroyer of Worlds." She shook her head. "Isn't that what the Hindus call Shiva?"

Mark felt dread fill his stomach. He looked over at Bill and he was scowling, his handsome face contorted in concern.

"Many, many years ago, there was a great battle between the forces of Light and the servants of Elspeth, Destroyer of Worlds," Bill intoned, as if sharing an ancient tale. Which he was, come to think of it. Mark knew it, but he knew Shelly had no clue.

"But Elspeth was banished to the forgotten realms, never to return," Mark said, looking at Bill now for confirmation.

"She was, but there have been signs… And incidents… All around the world." Bill shook his head. "Your kind have been reporting encounters with *Venifucus* agents for years now. We once thought that evil order had been eradicated for all time, but it's back. If it ever left. And then there are the tales of sea creatures the likes of which have not been seen in millennia. Some even say the leviathan itself has been loosed once more in our oceans, where it does not belong."

Mark frowned. He'd heard the stories too. Good intel, from people he trusted said all these things were true.

"*Venifucus*," Shelly said, drawing his attention. "That's the word Antony used as well. He said his position in the *Venifucus* would be assured if he completed his task, which was to kill Mark."

"I led this evil to your door," Mark realized with a sinking feeling. He wanted to crush her to him, but resisted. He had to apologize first and see if she would forgive him. "I'm so sorry, *mi amor.*"

"Don't be silly." Shelly dismissed his heartache with a casual wave, making his inner cat want to growl in amusement. She was such an unpredictable female. He would enjoy the next decades getting to know her moods. "After the incident at the hotel," she went on talking to her father. "I came straight home and didn't leave again until after Mark had convinced me to go on a site visit."

"Site visit? You're asking her to design something for you?" Bill asked, clearly intrigued.

"It's a project for the Clan," was all Mark would say for now. He was still feeling this man out, although his instincts said Bill was okay. Still, Mark was cautious when it came to the safety of his people. "Let me just go out there and check on the cavalry," Mark said, rising from the couch. He didn't want to, but he really did have to pass on the warning about not touching the body, otherwise his people or their allies among the wolves might run into trouble. With Antony confirmed as having been a highly-placed *Venifucus* agent, they would have to be doubly cautious in dealing with what was left of him.

CHAPTER 13

When Mark had left the room and the house, Shelly met her father's eyes. "Are you okay with this?" she asked, getting it out in the open. "With him?"

Her dad gave a genuine sigh that held what sounded to her like relief.

"Frankly, I'm pleased. Although I could wish he was a little less of a target himself. Then again, I saw what he did to that mage out there. He can protect you. That's all I've ever wanted for you—someone who could love you and keep you safe once I'm gone."

"Dad! Don't talk like that. You're not going anywhere." She couldn't imagine a world without him in it.

"But it's the reality I've been dealing with for years now. Every one of our family is gone. We're all that's left of the once-proud Howells." He shook his head. "I've fought more battles in the past few years than most people fight in a lifetime. Those with evil intent are constantly at me, trying to subdue me and steal my power. So far, they haven't succeeded. But my worst fear is that, someday, someone will best me, and you'll be left unprotected. Which is why I'm more than okay with you and Mark Pepard." He sat forward and gave her a level stare. "If he's serious."

"Oh, I'm serious." This time, it was Mark who had come

into the conversation unannounced. He sat next to Shelly and placed a protective arm around her. "I'm as serious as a jaguar can be. Shelly is my mate. I'm just having a little trouble convincing her of exactly what that means."

Her dad's grin was instant and wide. "Well, then, I have no objection. Welcome to the family, Mark." He reached out a hand across the small coffee table, and Mark met him halfway. Both men were smiling as if the union was a *fait acompli*.

"What? Just like that?" Shelly tried to object, but the men were still grinning.

"Give her time to figure it out," her father advised Mark. "She only just discovered magic, after all. It'll take time to learn about her fey heritage."

Mark sat back with a stunned look on his face. "Fey? That's where your magic comes from?"

Her dad shrugged. "Some of it. There were a lot of human mages mixed in over the years, but the fey blood breeds true in almost every case. Shelly's always had it. It's just been bottled up inside her, unable to find a way out." He was looking at her fondly, but his words were directed to Mark. "Have you seen the sparks?"

Mark nodded. "Fire mage was the guess of my *abuela*. The first time they appeared, we were in the caldera of an inactive volcano."

Her dad's eyes widened in surprise. *Good.* She'd managed to surprise him. Even if they were talking about her as if she wasn't even sitting right there in front of them.

"You don't say? Now that sounds like an interesting location, and the exact spot destined for a fire mage to ignite."

"*Abuela* said just about the same thing," Mark agreed. "One thing I'm curious about…"

"Just one thing?" Bill replied, clearly amused.

"Your daughter accepted the existence of shifters with ease, but any time the conversation turned toward magic, she seemed to hit a wall of disbelief. As if she couldn't believe the evidence of her own eyes or was in denial for some reason." Mark's gaze narrowed. "I don't think it was natural and I'm wondering if you had something to do with her aversion."

Bill sat back, an appraising look on his face that turned quickly to one of respect as he nodded. "I am an expert at casting wards…and other spells. Once I realized Shelly had been born latent, I devised multiple strategies around keeping her safe. One of those was to cast a spell that would keep her from believing in magic—not the fairy stories of children's fantasies. I couldn't deny her those gifts of childhood. But *real* magic. I didn't want her looking too closely at that sort of thing because I never wanted her to feel badly about herself for not being able to access the magic that was her heritage. It wasn't her fault, after all. Latency happens, even in the best of families."

Well that was news to her. Too bad he hadn't thought to be honest with her. Shelly thought her life would have been a lot different—and her relationship with her father much closer—had he trusted her with the truth. It would take her some time to come to terms with his decisions, but she already knew she would forgive him. No matter how misguided, he'd done everything he'd done out of a desire to keep her safe.

He loved her. It was clear in the extraordinary lengths he'd gone to, trying to make her life as secure as possible.

The men went on discussing the finer aspects of everything that had happened for a while, but eventually, Shelly started to yawn. It had been a hell of a long day with too much excitement. She was about to crash, and crash hard.

Apparently, her father noticed. "Well, it's the middle of the night," he said, looking at his watch. "I'd better be going."

"Nonsense," she said quickly. "It's too late for you to be out roaming around on your own. I want everyone I care about safe for a little while. You can have the guest room."

"Circling the wagons, eh?" her father asked shrewdly, but gave in. "All right. I see the sense in that for now. I have my go bag in the Rolls. I'll just go get it."

"Go bag?" Mark asked as her dad left the room again and she stood from the couch. He followed her up and put both arms loosely around her waist. "Your father keeps a go bag in his Rolls?"

She nodded. "He always has. Ever since I can remember. He's got overnight bags in every vehicle he owns."

"So do most shifters, but that's because we always need to find extra clothes if we damage or leave our original outfit somewhere else. Can't just walk around naked in the human world."

With a body like his, she couldn't imagine why not, but she kept that thought carefully to herself, considering that her father might walk back in at any time. Instead, she leaned into Mark's warmth.

"Did I thank you yet for saving me tonight?" she whispered to him, her lips yearning toward his.

"You had a lot to do with the saving, *querida*. If you ask me, it was a joint effort," he told her.

"That's mighty generous of you, Mister Alpha," she told him teasingly. Drunk on relief, now that the battle was over and everyone was safe.

He chuckled. "It's just Alpha. And to you, it's just Mark. Or my beloved, or any other endearment you want to call me. I'm yours, *mi amor*, forevermore."

"Mmm. I'm beginning to like the sound of that," she told him, just starting to dare to believe that magic was real and this…thing…this explosive attraction between them might be more than just a passing fancy.

Mark looked serious, and her father seemed all too ready to take him at face value. If her dad believed Mark wouldn't walk away after he'd had his fun, then perhaps he knew something she didn't.

What was she thinking? *Of course* her father knew something she didn't.

He'd known about magic his whole life, while she was a total novice. He probably knew a lot more about shifters than she had been able to learn in the short time she'd been in on the secret of their existence. Her dad probably knew all sorts of things about this *mating* thing among Mark's kind, even if Dad was something else.

Fey, he'd said. Mark had recognized that word—and understood what it had meant—on first hearing it. All Shelly knew was that the word was associated with fairies and magic and all things cute and sparkly. That probably wasn't very accurate. She'd have to hit up her dad for an explanation. Tomorrow. Her jaw cracked in another giant yawn. Definitely tomorrow.

When her head hit the pillow a few minutes later, she had barely taken the time to brush her teeth and put on a nightgown. There would be no pre-sleep nookie tonight, and Mark seemed okay with that. He was attentive and kind, helping her with her nightgown and not attempting to start anything she didn't have the strength to finish.

When she woke a few hours later, just before dawn, that was another story. Mark was up, his eyes glowing a little eerily in the darkness as he leaned up against the upholstered headboard. He was watching her sleep.

Immediately, her heart melted. He'd been watching over her. Her own personal guard jaguar, in a hunky human package. How could a girl get so lucky?

"Come here," she whispered, inviting him down into her embrace.

He didn't waste any time. Mark slid down the bed and joined her once more, flat on his back as she rose over him. She straddled him, climbing that handsome body—if not entirely gracefully, then at least with enthusiasm. It was easy to get enthusiastic about making love with Mark.

He was everything she ever could have dreamed of in a man...and more. So much more. The jaguar. The magic. The care, devotion and...love. Yes, love. She could feel it coming off him whenever they were near.

It was those instincts of hers again, telling her that this man would never hurt her. Not consciously. Not intentionally. No, he was all about protecting her. Cherishing her. *Loving* her.

And she realized in that moment… She loved him too.

At some point, while she hadn't been paying attention, everything had changed. Love had blossomed in her heart. A connection had formed between her soul and his. Never to be broken.

She loved him, and whether she was ready for it or not, she was committed to him in every way. She just hadn't gotten up the courage to admit it to herself until that moment.

She had to tell him. She had to see his reaction. She had to know if her instincts were right again.

Shelly stilled on top of him, her hands on his shoulders as she looked down to meet his gaze. The best way was the simple way, she thought.

"I love you, Mark," she whispered, looking deep into his eyes.

The spark of joy that lit his gaze from within contained not just the human side, but also the inner jaguar looking out at her. Both of them were happy. One might even say triumphant.

Mark's hands tightened on her waist.

"I love you with all my heart, Shelly. And I always will." His declaration was both sweet and compelling. "Do you agree to be my mate? My wife? My life's companion?"

"Yes, to all three," she answered with a smile she couldn't contain. It filled her heart, her soul, and every fiber of her being.

She kissed him then, and it went quickly from sweet and joyful to fiery and passionate. She lowered herself onto him, wanting complete union between their bodies while her spirit soared with his, in perfect alignment. They would have years to hone their rhythm and the way they complemented each other, but this moment out of time was…just right.

And then, he began to move. Impatience seemed to be the rule of the day when he rolled them over until he could control the motion. She was happy to oblige since she'd lost control over her limbs at some point while the earth was shattering a bit beneath her.

She could feel magic stirring in her soul, and her fingers were tingling. Her last coherent thought was that she hoped she didn't singe her pretty cotton sheets, but then again...who cared? They could buy more.

Mark drove her to peak after peak, thrusting and sliding within her in just the right way. He was her master in those moments, and she his willing slave, although... Mark seemed to be taking his cues from her moans of pleasure, a servant to her every whim, her every whimper of delight. So, who really was the master here? And did it really matter?

As they rocketed to the stars together, she decided it didn't matter one bit. The only thing that counted was that they were in love. Joined as one. As close as two people could be, and on the precipice of a life filled with laughter, luck and love the likes of which the world had never seen.

They made love again and again before finally rising for the day. There was still work to do, and as Shelly emerged from her bedroom, she heard her father moving around downstairs. Blushing a bit at the late hour, she realized he'd be fully aware of what they'd been doing all morning.

She'd never been in quite this situation before. Her father had never been present when she emerged from any love nest where she'd been having raging sex with someone only a half hour before. She wasn't sure how to handle it.

"Want me to go first?" Mark asked, coming up behind her. "I have a few things I'd like to talk to him about, anyway. Why don't you go to your studio? I'll give you a shout when lunch is ready, okay?" He kissed her on top of her head in a gentle sign of affection.

"You're my hero," she whispered, taking what was quite possibly the coward's way out and making a beeline for her studio.

She heard Mark go down the stairs and greet her father, but she didn't linger, not wanting to hear any possible confrontation. Mark was a big boy. He could handle her father. Maybe.

True to his word, a short while later, Mark called her downstairs for lunch. Her dad greeted her normally, no raised eyebrows or knowing looks, thank the Goddess. He simply talked with Mark about the werewolves that apparently were patrolling outside her house.

"I've had dealings with Cassius and his brother many times over the years," her father was saying.

She knew from an earlier part of the conversation that he was naming the Midtown Alpha and his younger brother, Cassius. Mark had told her that Cassius was the one who had led the group that had saved her bacon at the hotel.

"I knew his mother, of course. She was a lovely young witch, who had a talent for the earth elements and growing things. Rather natural, I thought, when she mated with a werewolf," her father went on as they all sat down for lunch together.

They were dining on a meal delivered by one of Mark's people a short while before. Mark had arranged catering for everyone involved in this operation, renting out a place just down the road for the security contingent where they could sleep, shower, eat and generally be well treated between shifts up here at Shelly's house.

It wasn't an ideal solution for anything long term, but it would work for now. Mark took good care of his people, and he wouldn't eat gourmet food without offering the same to his staff. Shelly loved his egalitarian outlook and realized, all over again, how perfect they were for each other.

"I didn't know he had a magical side," Mark observed as they ate.

"It's not something they advertise, I understand, but Cassius, at least, definitely inherited some of his mother's considerable skills. He hasn't trained them the way he should, of course. It's been somewhat difficult for him, from what I can gather. His Pack doesn't have a great deal of trust in human magic, and his mother was an earth mage of the highest caliber. A true servant of the Light. I was saddened when she was killed."

They were silent a moment, almost in observation of respect for the fallen. They continued to eat the delicious meal Mark's people had provided, and eventually, Mark spoke again.

"Bill, there is one thing I wanted to ask you about those wards of yours."

"Certainly," her dad replied, looking like he'd be willing to divulge his secrets—up to a point.

"I was wondering if you'd be willing to cast a ward around our new home…on Jaguar Island."

"Jaguar Island?" Bill tilted his head in question.

"That's what we renamed it when my Clan bought the place last year," Mark told him. "It's the dormant volcano where your daughter's power first sprang to life. It's to be the new Clan home for all jaguars, if they want to come. I won't force anybody, but the idea is that it will be a place where we can come together as a Clan and rebuild. There are few of us left in the world now, and I want to try to change that."

"A noble cause," Bill said gravely as he smoothed his napkin. "And now that the fate of the Howells is linked to the fate of your Clan, I can tell you that my skills are completely at your disposal. Though I hope you will understand that I never had an Alpha, so I probably won't be the most obedient of subordinates… If that's the role you want me to fulfill."

"Never that, Bill. I'm not a monarch like the other big cat shifters. I'm not even a Lord like the *were* Tribes seem to enjoy. I'm just an Alpha with a widely scattered Clan, trying to rebuild." Mark was a lot more than that, and they all knew it, but he was a good man who didn't wield his power like a weapon.

"There are a certain group of elders in the Clan who keep their own counsel and help pass the knowledge we need down to the younger generation. They are our conscience and our barometer. They are the counsel I seek when I need to make the big decisions. I rather thought that's the kind of role you'd fit into. If you want it."

Mark's demeanor was off-hand, but Shelly knew this was a big offer. Very big. To bring an outsider—a mage who didn't have a jaguar in his soul—into the heart of the Clan was a step even Shelly understood to be huge.

Her dad smiled a soft, genuine smile, and there was a sparkle in his eyes that spoke of high emotion. "I think I'd like that. You honor me, Alpha."

They continued their lunch together and discussed wedding plans a bit, then Bill got the low-down about the island, and Shelly told them both about her ideas for the structures they would build there. She had big dreams about things they would construct years into the future.

There was a lot of work to be done on Jaguar Island, and she was just the architect to do it. The Clan home would be her life's work. Her greatest achievement. And her labor of love.

After all, the fate of the Clan and of the Howell bloodline was in her hands now. She hoped at least one of her children would have mage powers, and that her father would have a chance to pass on his knowledge. Shelly herself feared she had come into her power too late in life to ever really master it, but she'd do what she could. For her father's sake, she would pray for at least one true mage of her blood for him to teach in the years ahead.

As for the rest... If they were going to rebuild the Clan, Shelly was looking forward to having lots of Mark's babies...and all the fun they would have making them.

Good thing she'd always wanted a large family.

A few days later, after things had settled down and Shelly had packed her things and sealed up her house for an extended vacation, she and Mark set sail on his private yacht. Their eventual destination was Jaguar Island, but they were taking the scenic route in order to enjoy a little bit of a honeymoon before the big mating party his people were already planning.

Shelly was involved in some of the preparations via a state-of-the-art satellite communications center on the huge boat. She spent a few minutes each day looking at dress designs and color schemes and working with Marie and Janice on the menu remotely. She was enjoying planning a bit of the big party but was more than willing to let others do the work.

They all seemed so happy to put on this special occasion for her—and their Alpha. She was happy to let them do their worst, knowing that she and Mark would have to have a more traditional ceremony and reception in a few months on the mainland, in order to make their marriage legal in the eyes of the human world they lived in.

He'd also discussed his penchant for leaking photographs to the tabloids to earn extra money for the Clan. Shelly had laughed at the sneakiness of it all. Just like a cat, she thought.

She would have a big society wedding. Not because she really wanted that sort of pomp and circumstance—though what girl didn't secretly dream of a fairytale wedding when she was little?

No, the wedding would be more about putting on a show for the humans. Solidifying their relationship for the press. And networking with the hundreds who would be invited from the business community.

It would be a dream and a sham all at the same time, but it would be worth it. If it would help the Clan, she was all for it. She also knew it would help her father and what remained of the Howell reputation, which was a nice added benefit.

In fact, her father was already reaping the rewards of their new connection. He'd been able to reclaim some of the money he'd put aside for Shelly's security into the future. He'd also rebuilt ties with the Midtown werewolf Pack. In a town as densely populated as Manhattan, it was good to have strong allies, and Shelly rested easier knowing her father wasn't all alone out there with nobody to help him if he should come under magical attack.

For now, though, she was all about sailing off into the sunset with her mate. They had a few days until they got to the island and the big party. She was determined to make the most of them…with the loving, magical Alpha of her very own.

# # #

Thank you for reading **The Jaguar Tycoon**. If you enjoyed this book, please consider leaving a review. The next book in the series is **The Jaguar Bodyguard.**

If you want to read more about the tiger king, Mitch, and his mate, Gina, check out their book, **King's Throne**, now available.

Howls Romance
Classic romance... with a furry twist!

Did you enjoy this Howls Romance story?

If YES, check out the other books in the Howls Romance line by heading over to our website! HowlsRomance.com.

ABOUT THE AUTHOR

Bianca D'Arc has run a laboratory, climbed the corporate ladder in the shark-infested streets of lower Manhattan, studied and taught martial arts, and earned the right to put a whole bunch of letters after her name, but she's always enjoyed writing more than any of her other pursuits. She grew up and still lives on Long Island, where she keeps busy with an extensive garden, several aquariums full of very demanding fish, and writing her favorite genres of paranormal, fantasy and sci-fi romance.

Bianca loves to hear from readers and can be reached through Twitter (@BiancaDArc), Facebook (BiancaDArcAuthor) or through the various links on her website.

WELCOME TO THE D'ARC SIDE…
WWW.BIANCADARC.COM

OTHER BOOKS BY BIANCA D'ARC

Brotherhood of Blood
One & Only
Rare Vintage
Phantom Desires
Sweeter Than Wine
Forever Valentine
Wolf Hills*
Wolf Quest

Tales of the Were
Lords of the Were
Inferno

Tales of the Were ~
The Others
Rocky
Slade

Tales of the Were ~
String of Fate
Cat's Cradle
King's Throne
Jacob's Ladder
Her Warriors

Tales of the Were ~
Redstone Clan
The Purrfect Stranger
Grif
Red
Magnus
Bobcat
Matt

Tales of the Were ~
Grizzly Cove
All About the Bear
Mating Dance
Night Shift
Alpha Bear
Saving Grace
Bearliest Catch
The Bear's Healing Touch
The Luck of the Shifters
Badass Bear

Tales of the Were ~
Were-Fey Love Story
Lone Wolf
Snow Magic
Midnight Kiss

Tales of the Were ~
Jaguar Island (Howls)
The Jaguar Tycoon
The Jaguar Bodyguard

Gemini Project
Tag Team
Doubling Down

Resonance Mates
Hara's Legacy**
Davin's Quest
Jaci's Experiment
Grady's Awakening
Harry's Sacrifice

Dragon Knights

Daughters of the Dragon
Maiden Flight*
Border Lair
The Ice Dragon**
Prince of Spies***

Dragon Knights ~ Novellas
The Dragon Healer
Master at Arms
Wings of Change

Sons of Draconia
FireDrake
Dragon Storm
Keeper of the Flame
Hidden Dragons

The Sea Captain's Daughter
Book 1: Sea Dragon
Book 2: Dragon Fire
Book 3: Dragon Mates

Guardians of the Dark
Half Past Dead
Once Bitten, Twice Dead
A Darker Shade of Dead
The Beast Within
Dead Alert

StarLords
Hidden Talent
Talent For Trouble
Shy Talent

Jit'Suku Chronicles ~ Arcana
King of Swords
King of Cups
King of Clubs
King of Stars
End of the Line
Diva

Jit'Suku Chronicles ~ Sons of Amber
Angel in the Badlands
Master of Her Heart

StarLords
Hidden Talent
Talent For Trouble
Shy Talent

Gifts of the Ancients
Warrior's Heart

* RT Book Reviews Awards Nominee
** EPPIE Award Winner
*** CAPA Award Winner

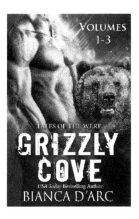

The first three Grizzly Cove stories in one place!

Welcome to Grizzly Cove, where bear shifters can be who they are - if the creatures of the deep will just leave them be. Wild magic, unexpected allies, a conflagration of sorcery and shifter magic the likes of which has not been seen in centuries... That's what awaits the peaceful town of Grizzly Cove. That, and love. Lots and lots of love.

This anthology contains:

All About the Bear
Welcome to Grizzly Cove, where the sheriff has more than the peace to protect. The proprietor of the new bakery in town is clueless about the dual nature of her nearest neighbors, but not for long. It'll be up to Sheriff Brody to clue her in and convince her to stay calm—and in his bed—for the next fifty years or so.

Mating Dance
Tom, Grizzly Cove's only lawyer, is also a badass grizzly bear, but he's met his match in Ashley, the woman he just can't get out of his mind. She's got a dark secret, that only he knows. When ugliness from her past tracks her to her new home, can Tom protect the woman he is fast coming to believe is his mate?

Night Shift
Sheriff's Deputy Zak is one of the few black bear shifters in a colony of grizzlies. When his job takes him into closer proximity to the lovely Tina, though, he finds he can't resist her. Could it be he's finally found his mate? And when adversity strikes, will she turn to him, or run into the night? Zak will do all he can to make sure she chooses him.

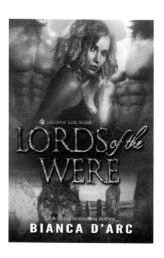

Allie is about to discover a heritage of power…and blood…werecreatures, magic, and a misguided vampire who wants to kill two men who could be the loves of her life.

Allie was adopted. She had always known it, but when a mysterious older woman shows up and invites her to learn about her birth family, things take a turn for the odd.

Then Allie meets the Lords. Twin Alpha werewolves who rule over all North American were, Rafe and Tim may look exactly alike, but Allie can tell them apart from the moment they first meet. She's not sure what to think when they both want to claim her as their mate.

They are dominant, sexy, and all too ready to play games of the most delicious kind with her, but when a rogue vampire threatens her safety, they jump to her defense. It will take all of them working together, to stop the evil that has invaded their territory. Can they trust in each other and the power of their new love to prevail? Or will an ancient enemy win the day and usher evil incarnate back into the world?

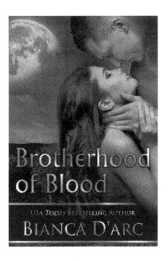

The first three novellas in the critically acclaimed vampire romance series, now in one place...

One & Only
Atticus is about to give up and greet the sun when he finds the love of his eternal life...by accident.

Rare Vintage
Marc, Master vampire of the Napa Valley, can't keep away from Kelly, no matter how many sparks fly between them. When an enemy challenges his authority, will she sacrifice her life for his?

Phantom Desires
Master Dmitri's lair is located under a farmhouse in rural Wyoming. Spying on the new owner while she sleeps could be more dangerous than even he suspects.

WWW.BIANCADARC.COM

Made in the USA
San Bernardino, CA
24 January 2018